I0592689

SHADOWS OF DOUBT

PART ONE OF THE EMERALD TABLET: BOOK
ONE OF THE CHRONICLES OF THE
SUPERNATURAL

JM HART

JMH WORLD PUBLISHING

ABOUT SHADOWS OF DOUBT

PART ONE OF THE EMERALD TABLET BOOK ONE IN THE
CHRONICLES OF THE SUPERNATURAL

A shape-shifting plague. A group of supernatural teens.
Can they control their untested gifts to prevent
annihilation?

According to her religious guardian, Sophia has been
blessed with a mission from God. But the orphaned girl
would rather go dancing with friends than witness
prophecies about the coming apocalypse. When she
discovers six other teens struggling to harness their
superhuman gifts, she knows she has no choice but to
unite the group against a swarm of evil.

Despite awe-inspiring magical powers and inter-
dimensional travel at their fingertips, Sophia fears their
abilities won't be enough to preserve millions of innocent
lives.

Shadows of Doubt is part one of The Emerald Tablet an
action-packed paranormal Apocalyptic fantasy in The
Chronicles of The Supernatural filled with daring teens,
page-turning adventures, and otherworldly powers.

I dedicate this book to my daughter Bianca — never stop dreaming.

We know what we are, but know not what we may be.

William Shakespeare.

MEPHITIS PESTILENCE: SHAUN. ISRAEL

S haun moved his legs in a scissor motion, kicking his heels rhythmically against the boulder; he felt each impact pulse down his feet to his toes. He heard the vibrations of the red string protecting the excavated sites being plucked by the same wind blowing the sand off the tips of the dunes. The area, empty of working archaeologists, was eerily quiet. Shaun imagined the sand spirits whispering, moving like ghosts in the sun's glare. Ignoring his fear he started humming, mimicking the resonance of the red string.

He'd been desperate to accompany his father on a dig such as this one, but it wasn't turning out as he'd imagined. Each time he'd begged his dad to go, he'd been told, "You're too young! When you're older; Mom needs you." His dad had promised to take him on adventures Shaun read about in books, but Shaun felt the emptiness of those promises. Sensing his mother's pain and hopelessness, he'd craved to escape the dark cloud that enveloped her.

Then, after only a few days back home in Australia after his dad had been gone for weeks, he had told him, "I believe I've found a cure for your mother; though I have to leave one more time." However this time, he'd been forced to take Shaun with him.

Shaun was wishing he was home at his mom's bedside. He closed his eyes and imagined he was resting his head on her chest. He could smell the perfumed air of her room and feel the gentle stroke of her hand on his head as she softly hummed a tune. Hours had passed since his dad and the other archaeologists had disappeared into the cave. He was in awe of his dad, but scared of him at the same time. Feeling dread creep up on him, he shivered, shifted on the boulder and pitched stones at the trucks, pretending he wasn't anxious. The red desert behind him gave him the jitters big-time. He was glad he had company, even if it was a girl: Rachel, the daughter of the head archaeologist, his dad's boss. She was sitting next to him on the boulder, chewing the ends of her long, wavy black hair. Rachel sat scanning the desert mountains that faced the distant blue haze of the Dead Sea. He followed her eyes, watching them double back to the track that was covered with sand and stone. It snaked down and around the side of the mountain, to the caves where their fathers had gone. To distract her he gave her half of his sandwich. She flattened the bread, squashing the slices together.

Earlier in the day, Shaun had seen her hiding on the back of one of the trucks. He'd spotted her peeking out from under the tarpaulin. He'd watched her as she cautiously wriggled over the side and jumped off. Seeing him, she'd frozen, knitted her eyebrows together pleadingly and put a finger up to her lips to beg him to stay silent. She must've sensed he wasn't a threat, because she'd suddenly slid under the truck like a baseball player sliding into home plate, and as soon as the archaeologists had left, she'd just as quickly — like a lizard — crawled out from under the truck and run after them.

Shaun had sprinted after her. He'd found she was taller than him, and fast, but he was faster. *She must be at least a year older,* he'd thought as he got closer; *at least eight.* She'd been wearing hiking boots and a pretty lilac floral dress that was covered with smudges of dirt. Shaun had grabbed her by the arm, and she'd jerked to a stop at the entrance to the cave. He wanted to stop her following the men. He'd been afraid she'd get lost; mostly, however, what he'd really feared was being alone in the desert.

Rachel had shaken her arm free and stared fiercely into his face. He'd brushed his straight, sweaty dark hair out of his eyes. She'd looked back down into the mysterious cave. They could no longer hear her father or the other men. In a display of fiery anger she'd ranted and raved in her own language, waved her arms about madly, and stomped on his shoe.

She'd then suddenly stopped to size him up, tilting her head to the left, then the right and then back again, as if she was trying to work out what the image in an abstract painting was meant to be.

Shaun thought she looked at him as if there was something unusual about him. Whatever she'd been thinking passed and she smiled. "Rachel," she said with a heavy accent.

A truce. "Shaun."

Together they now waited in silence for their fathers to return. Hours had passed. At first, they hadn't noticed the time going by, because they'd quickly amused themselves, playing games as if they'd been friends forever. They'd enjoyed seeing who could jump further, run faster and throw higher. They'd taken a large piece of cardboard from a box in the truck and sat on it to race down the side of the dune. Eventually, they'd tired of climbing back up to the top. Shaun was now growing restless seeing the sky turning black.

In the valley, the nights were cold and the days hot. Shaun could feel a wind blowing in from the west and thought of how this day was a spiritual one for the locals. He could clearly hear the sound of the ram's horn calling across the land, from Metzoke Dragot, or maybe from as far afield as Ein Gedi. He loves the name, it sounds like Jedi. The wind whipped the sand against his legs. He watched Rachel jumping down from the rock, her long hair flowing behind her as she turned towards the golden sand dune. Having been perched on the boulder for so long, Shaun realized his bum was getting sore and his feet were throbbing from kicking against the rock. He stood up on the rock to scan the area, looking for any sign of his father, before he slid down to the ground.

They both shivered as the final light of the sun, and the first light of the moon was swallowed up in darkness.

Shaun noticed Rachel had become tense, and although they didn't speak the same language, he could tell something was wrong. He felt himself shiver again, chilled by the frightening howling of the red string mixed with the distant bellow of the horn. He watched as Rachel pointed to her right, up into the distant sky, where the stars were twinkling brightly, arching off the horizon and up to the heavens. He saw the left part of the sky was empty, nothing but darkness: no stars shined, they were blanketed by a dirty haze, a sandstorm.

He and Rachel began to cough and choke, and he could feel the sand biting at his face and neck. *The dust spirits have whipped up around us. Any air that was in the valley has been squashed!* He thought.

Rachel tucked her chin into her dress to cover her mouth, and shouted to Shaun, in muffled broken English, "Quick! Come!" She reached for his hand and motioned to him to start running for the cave; they stopped just inside the mouth.

"Papa! *Papa!*" Rachel shouted into the darkness.

The wind was now blowing at their backs, pushing them forward.

Shaun dug into the pockets of his Levis, searching for his miniature blue LED light. It was a gift from his mother, she'd given it to him the last time she'd been admitted to hospital. She had pulled it out from under her pillow and pressed it into his hand and mumbled, "Turn on ... no darkness. Thoughts make merry-go-rounds. We ... thoughts control; control thoughts. She will live." He'd felt sad and embarrassed to hear the jumbled words. He hadn't understood what she had said, later his dad had explained that the medicine had taken hold and she was no longer coherent.

Shaun flicked the torch on and stepped further into the cave, feeling his throat being scratched by thick, coarse air. Cupping his hand around his mouth, he yelled as loudly as he could, "*Dad!*"

They sensed the echoes penetrating the earth and traveling under the ancient land towards Mount Zion. They waited, afraid to move.

"*Dad!*" Shaun repeated. Still no reply.

They walked a bit further in from the entrance, away from the storm, deeper into the old caves. Shaun ran his left hand along the grooved wall, then inhaled sharply and shook his hand in pain. Droplets of blood, like beads, had formed in chains across his palm. It stung like gravel rash. Shaun rubbed the granules of sand and blood on his jeans. "The air's so gritty," he said.

Scared and alone, they crouched against the wall and waited. Shaun pointed the torch towards the ceiling, trying not to shine the light in Rachel's face. They looked at each other, wearing fake smiles to mask their fears. Outside, the storm was raging; inside the cave was deathly silent.

Rachel began to cry and whispered a prayer.

Shaun watched as her mouth moved, but couldn't understand a word she was saying. *Her eyes are emeralds.* His dad had given his mom a pair of emerald earrings, but she'd never worn them; they'd stayed a sparkle hidden inside her jewelry box.

He pulled out his Swiss army knife and started drawing in the dirt.

Rachel watched him and slowly picked up a rock to use to finish his pictures of spiral galaxies, joining them together with strong lines into the shape of a kite.

The pitch-blackness of the cave was eased by the glow of the light from his mother's torch.

The sandstorm began to pass, hard rain started to fall, and their hiding place became illuminated by quick bursts of lightning.

Shaun's concern that something was wrong increased. He knew his dad hadn't planned to be gone for so long. Early that morning, Shaun had woken to the tapping sounds of typing. He'd stayed under his bedcovers and had watched his dad on the laptop, booking the flights for tomorrow. They were to head home, back to mom. His dad had been unusually happy and excited, and while Shaun had been picking the sleep out of his eyes, his dad had come over, sat beside him and said, "After today, we'll be able to afford — and provide — all the good health your mother needs. We'll have the tablet."

Rachel moved closer to him, breaking his train of thought. He could smell her hair and see the worry on her face. Both of them were hungry, cold and tired. Bit by bit, Rachel nudged closer, until they were huddling together.

Shaun started to hum a tune his mom had sung whenever he was afraid of a thunderstorm. In the empty cave, his voice sounded delicate and shaky.

With her head on his shoulder, Rachel soon floated off into a restless sleep. Shaun was surprised he wasn't grossed out, her being a girl and all. At school, the girls were trouble, with their giggling and whispering, but Rachel seemed different.

He began to drift into sleep...

Something probed his mind — a distant sound. He

surfaced to consciousness and sat wide-eyed, straining to hear. He gagged, registering a repulsive smell floating in from one of the tunnels like the smell at the garbage tip. He covered his nose and mouth, his eyes watering as the stench grew stronger.

He felt Rachel jolt as if her senses were rocked by the sickly vapors too. On the tail of the stench came the faint sound of screaming, mayhem unfolding, as the odor got closer and stronger. He heard the painful cries of men, as if from a distant battlefield, being amplified from the depths of the cave. As suddenly as the noises of suffering and torture had arisen, they ceased.

Shaun was paralyzed. He stared hard into the tunnel, squinting in an effort to penetrate the murkiness beyond the light of his torch. He bit down on his lower lip, drawing blood. He stood, and shuffled one step forward. The density of the blackness intensified, expanding like oil. It seemed to be moving towards him.

His saliva tasted metallic as if he'd been chewing his necklace and its dangling silver scorpion. He went to spit in the dirt but was stopped mid-spit by an explosion of harsh sound. Slowly he wiped his mouth. Shaun heard a corrosive shrilling within the labyrinth of tunnels. The unbearable screeches pierced his skull and reverberated in his mind. They clamped their hands tightly over their ears to block the noise that sounded like a swarm of tiny-metallic claws being dragged along the cave's walls. A message was sent to every part of his mind and body: a signal to run, to scream — anything to escape.

He saw the dense mass move like a snake towards them. He could barely move his thumb over the torch's black-rubber button to turn it off. The screeching grew louder. Rachel screamed, and Shaun quickly slapped his hand over her mouth. He saw her eyes were wide and filled with horror. He heard his heart pounding in his ears and felt fear crawling up his spine; out of the corner of his eye, he could see a shimmer of reflective light, like a flock of birds high in a sun-filled sky. That's when he saw the semi-transparent flying creatures, although he wished to God he hadn't. They had gilled necks, masses of bubbling lesions on their bat-like faces, vulturine feet, the jagged tail of a scorpion with a sharp arrow-tip, and the wings of a desolate angel. Within seconds, the faces resembling a bat's changed to a dog's snout ... the creatures were shapeshifting, constantly fluctuating and never completely forming. The air was like soup and the energy was suffocating; it had a vice-like grip around Shaun's throat.

The tiny beasts were fighting each other: pushing and shoving each other towards the entrance; tearing each other apart. They exploded from the mouth of the cave; a swarm of evil disappeared high into the dark sky. The cave fell silent. Light dancing off the walls was moving closer to them. Somebody coughed in the distance. "Who was that?" Shaun blurted out, looking at Rachel, quickly dropping the hand he had over her mouth. *She's going to cry,* he thought. *I have to protect her!* She looked how he felt: petrified.

They scurried to the other side of the cave and crouched behind a boulder. The silhouette of a man, with a backpack hanging off his shoulder, rushed past them and out into the night. He stood just beyond the entrance, coughing, "Shaun!" the man shouted. "Shaun, where are you?"

Shaun stood up and pulled at Rachel.

She wouldn't budge.

"Come on!" he whispered. "Let's go!"

Rachel didn't move; all she did was shake her head rapidly and move further out of sight.

Shaun stared at her and frowned. She shooed him away and began to cry silently, the tears marked her dirty cheeks. Their eyes met.

Despite the despair she must have been feeling, Rachel smiled.

Shaun smiled back, then turned and ran towards his father. "Dad! Dad!" he yelled. "I'm over here!" He wrapped his arms around his dad's waist and hugged him tightly. "Where are the others?" he asked him. "What happened? You were gone for so long!"

His father pushed him aside. "Stop talking."

He looked at his father's face that was screwed up with anger and hatred; a stranger's face. "But where are the rest?" he asked again.

His dad dropped the backpack at Shaun's feet and ran over to the truck. "There was an accident," he yelled back to Shaun as he lowered the tailgate and climbed on.

Shaun was glued to the spot. He watched his dad jump off the back of the truck carrying a wooden box and rush back to the cave, where he emptied the contents on the desert floor.

"They're not coming. Now, move! Pick up the backpack and get in the Jeep!"

Recognizing the symbols marked on the box, Shaun

felt he was going to wet his pants and vomit. He had such a strange feeling in his tummy he didn't know what to do. "That's dynamite!"

His dad just kept ignoring him and jamming the sticks into the cracks in the wall.

Shaun ran up to him and pulled at his belt to make him come away from the cave.

His dad slapped him hard, flinging him like a rag doll.

His face stung.

"Stop blubbering!" his father demanded as he wedged more explosives into every crack he could find. Then he set a timer.

Shaun jumped to his feet, bolted past his dad and yelled into the cave, "Rachel, get out! You have to get out!"

His dad knocked him to the ground then picked him up until they were eye to eye.

Shaun's face stung, and through his shirt he could feel his dad's fingernails. His dad's breath smelt stale and hot.

"Who the hell are you talking to?" he bellowed. "They're all gone! They're all dead!"

Shaun couldn't catch his breath. He started crying and couldn't stop. Suddenly he could see around his dad's head a cluster of parasites clashing with an invisible force field. Shaun became transfixed. *It's the tiny beasts.* He started to feel itchy all over. He wished his dad would put him back down on the ground. He could see the parasites were getting smaller as they move closer and closer to his father's head. One of them pierced the invisible force field, and the cluster streamed into his dad's left ear.

His dad, irritated, stretched his mouth so wide Shaun thought it would become unhinged. His dad became more anxious and angry, as if the parasites were urging him on.

Shaun leant back, away from his father's face. "What? The others can't be dead!" Shaun tried to pull away.

"What are you doing?" his dad yelled. He pulled him close, flipped him under his arm and used his other arm to pick up the backpack.

Shaun kicked and screamed, struggling to get down. His dad carried him to the Jeep and threw him into the back of the vehicle. Shaun heard the old Jeep grind into gear, and hung on to the seat as he looked back for Rachel. He saw the cave getting smaller and became afraid he'd lose sight of it. Then he saw Rachel emerge. As the vehicle bounced over the unsealed road, he willed Rachel to move: *Run, Rachel! Run!*

Frozen, she just stood there.

He continued watching and waiting for her to flee. He thought he saw her move away from the cave, towards him, and let his shoulders relax a bit. *She'll make it!* His dad was driving fast, and Rachel was getting further and further away. The sky was lit up by lightning, and in the distance, he thought he saw her raise her hand and wave. He raised his too, but the simple wave, the simple gesture, was lost: the cave exploded, and Rachel was no longer visible. The explosion was brighter than any of nature's fiery storms, brighter than any lightning bolt.

Shocked, Shaun allowed his hand to slowly drop. He didn't know what else to do, except cry.

"Turn around!" he heard his dad command him. "Wipe that stupid look off your face and open the luggage bag — quickly! Get the backpack! Reach in and you'll feel something wrapped up in cloth. I want you to take it out. It's heavy — be careful. But *don't* unwrap it! That's it!"

Shaun took some short, sharp breaths and felt his body jerking. He lifted an artifact out and tried to speak: "What ... what ... is ... is it?"

"Never you mind!" his dad replied. "Bury it among the clothes in the suitcase, and lock it!"

He felt the Jeep toss and turn, and twice he nearly dropped his dad's precious cargo. He did as he was told. The object was curved like a Roman chest plate covered with ancient writings and drawings. It was heavy and difficult to hold. Shaun struggled as he buried it deep in the suitcase and zipped it up. He used the back of his dirty hand to wipe the tears and snot from his face.

The Jeep screeched to a halt just outside the airport. His dad lifted the suitcase out, roughly turned Shaun around on the back seat, put the backpack over his shoulders. "Come on! Out of the car! Keep up! You're so weak it's pathetic! I've never noticed how soft you are — you're just like your mother!"

Shaun jumped out and, closing the door, spotted a leather pouch on the car floor. He picked it up and opened it slightly and saw oddly-shaped, multi-colored stones.

He PULLED the straps tight and shoved the pouch deep into his pocket and followed his father. Shaun hid his feelings behind the shadows of the night and as he ran to catch up, he felt the rain upon his face merge with the tears spilling down his cheeks. Everything seemed different. He was afraid.

Once inside the airport, his dad flashed Egyptian passports. They passed through Customs unquestioned and were allowed to board the plane immediately. Shaun sat next to the window and, looking around, saw the small plane was only half full. It shook and vibrated as it screamed down the runway. The storm had become violent, lightning hammered the tarmac. The ground shook with each strike, each blast reminding Shaun of the exploding cave. Some of the passengers screamed. He could see out the side window that the ground had cracked open. *Like a sinkhole*, he thought. The plane accelerated towards the hole and the lightning illuminated the crumbling ground. *We're not going to make it, we're not going to make it!* The heavy machine's wheels were inches from the abyss below them as the plane launched into the storm. The aircraft ascended into the terrifying turbulence created by the merciless clouds of micro- beasts released less than an hour ago from the cave. *They're following us.* It sounded as if the plane was being pelted with bullets.

As Shaun gripped the seat, his knuckles turned white. Oxygen masks sprang from their sockets. The plane continued its sharp rise to the heavens. They shot through the clouds and leveled out above the storm. They removed their oxygen masks and left them dangling. Shaun leant into his dad, "I'm scared."

"Everything'll be okay now, we have the tablet," his dad assured him. "Get some sleep; you want to be fresh to see your mother when we land."

Shaun felt exhausted, confused, frightened and mistrusting. "Dad, is Mom coming home? Is she better?"

HIS DAD DIDN'T ANSWER; he stared vacantly past him and out the window. Shaun shivered.

Shaun tried to sleep, but found himself tossing and turning in his seat, unable to stop thinking about Rachel...

"Wake up, boy!" he heard his dad demand. "Drink this!"

He saw his dad's eyes were black marbles — he was gone again. His dad shoved a clear plastic cup and a little yellow pill into Shaun's hands. He wanted to please his dad so he took the tablet.

Shaun fell into a deep sleep and awoke just before landing at home. He wanted to look out the window to see the beaches that stretched along the coast; he wanted to see the land of the sun and surf, his home — Australia. He felt groggy, and his body was heavy. He turned to his dad and saw him rummaging around in his backpack and wearing a different set of clothes. The couple sitting next to him unlocked their seat belts and reached up for the overhead compartments across the aisle. Shaun felt his empty stomach do a somersault and his head spun. There was no window; they were in the middle aisle, and it was six seats wide. *Where am I,* he wondered.

His dad looked at him, he heard him say something he couldn't understand as he handed over a vomit bag. *Perfect timing.* He buried his head in the waxed bag and puked. He came up for air, looked around the plane and saw it was full. That was when he realized he was on a different plane — a jumbo! He felt his dad pull him to his feet and push him into the aisle.

His head hurt. Everything was a blur as his dad kept him shuffling forward down the aisle, off the plane, and through Customs. Feeling fuzzy, and as if he was going to puke again, he tried hard to understand the Customs officer, who said to him, "Not much of a holiday for a young fella — a business trip to Dubai with your old man!" The man then handed back the two passports.

Shaun was focused on his passport, feeling confused. He fixated on its cover, the coat of arms. He ran his finger over the images of the kangaroo and emu: an Australian passport; his passport. *What happened to the Egyptian passports?* He looked up at his dad.

Noticing his perplexed look, his dad put his arm over Shaun's shoulders, as if he cared. "He's jetlagged and misses his mom," he said to the Customs officer.

That's true, Shaun thought.

They walked out of the airport, with the backpack only, not the suitcase.

"What about the suitcase?" Shaun asked his dad.

His father opened the door of the silver taxi and blankly asked, "What suitcase, son?"

Shaun climbed into the taxi and swore he'd never trust his dad again. *Was it all a dream?* They climbed into the back of the taxi. The air was so thick you could've cut it with a knife. Neither of them said a word as they headed for home.

2

TEN YEARS LATER: CASEY. UTAH, USA

Casey was skinny and had wild curly brown hair, and a tiny gap of prosperity between his two front teeth. He was tad short for his age, but he was a bright boy and was about to use parts of his mind Einstein would have only ever dreamed about.

He was walking home from school, happy. The wind was gathering strength and the leaves started spiraling around him and were swept up into the air and across the mountain road. Thunder echoed across the valley, heavy raindrops began to slap the sealed road. Like paint flung from the brush of an angry painter, dark clouds suddenly blacked out the sun. He shivered. Something was terribly wrong — there was an atmosphere of foreboding, and a churning sensation in the pit of his stomach.

The rain multiplied, and the howling wind pushed it diagonally across the deserted road. He peered into the dense forest, towards the shortcut, thinking of how it always looked downright eerie. He decided he'd stay on the road, but an uneasy feeling crept up his spine. He shouldered his schoolbag and started jogging.

He felt his woolen school blazer become heavy because it was soaking up the rain like an old sponge. It was two sizes too big, but his mom had said he'd "grow into it". Casey knew she'd felt bad about having to buy it from the school's seconds shop, but he also knew the scholarship hadn't included the cost of his school clothes. He didn't care, not really, and especially not today, because today was his thirteenth birthday and he was officially a teen.

The wind pushed him backward, and he could no longer see the road through the heavy rain. He had to go into the woods to get home quickly. He wouldn't think about the spooky stories the other kids told; he had to get home to his mom. She was alone, and the storm looked as if it was going to get bad really fast.

Casey darted off the road down the slippery embankment and entered the woods. He distracted himself by imagining his mom baking a delicious mud cake. He held the vision within his mind, his senses filled with the smell of warm chocolate. His mouth started to water and his tummy rumbled as he pictured the warm glow of the kitchen light and cooling cake. He smiled. It was as if the clouds had opened up above and a summer sun was now shining down on him. He continued to battle the rain, feeling washed with new energy.

Ignoring the whack of the squeaking "WARNING!" sign as it banged against the barbed-wire fence post, Casey crouched down under the wire, ran through the first stand of trees and headed for the stream, which on any other day would have been placid. *The kids never mentioned a "warning" sign,* he thought, *maybe this was a bad idea.*

He seemed to have jogged for a long time before he spotted the entrance to a footbridge. Its wooden entry posts were covered with green moss that was only half-concealing the termites. *Nobody uses it regularly!* he thought. *All the stories were lies!*

Having come too far to go back, he timidly held on to the worn rope balustrade and carefully put his weight down on the first plank. He rocked back and forth to test its strength. The other side of the bridge was cloaked in sheets of rain.

He sensed something moving behind him. *What was that?* He turned around quickly, checked behind himself, and saw a little off to the right was a storm water drain; the wire mesh covering its entrance was torn away. The gap was wide enough for someone — or something — to pass through. He started to freak out, and his conscious-ness started to flood with a medley of schoolyard stories. He pushed his wet hair out of his eyes, as if he were able to push the images away.

He stared past the rain and into the dark tunnel, but he couldn't see beyond its entrance. He strained to hear anything above the rain. Usually Casey loved the fresh smell of rain, but not today: he smelt something metallic in the air and a terrible taste in his mouth.

The thunderclaps continued shifting; moving closer. He looked down, between the slats of wood, and checked under the bridge. Although he knew it would be impossible for a meaty claw to pull him into the depths of a beast's lair, he couldn't help looking — just in case. The bridge was old and neglected, and when he stepped forward, he heard the pillars moan. Feeling unsure, he looked for another way across. Everything looked grey and lifeless, the color had been sucked out of the day and there was no golden light, no summer sun.

The stream below was a raging body of water. Knowing he had to move, Casey held his breath while testing the next plank. He kept going, never putting both his feet on the same plank at the same time. He pushed on into the wind.

When he reached the middle of the narrow footbridge, the wind lifted the whole bridge up as if it were a sail. Casey held tight on to the side ropes. The strong gust of wind dissipated and dropped the bridge back down. Seizing the moment, he pulled himself along, feeling the old rope fraying in his hands.

The heavens released their fury on him. Hail slammed into his backpack and into his shoulders, arms and head. He let go of the ropes and raised his arm to protect his head. He imagined his nightmarish phantom was under the bridge waiting for the last sliver of light to vanish. The bridge swayed dangerously.

When the hail stopped suddenly, he reached for the rope, but the wind drove him back. He pulled his heavy blazer tight around himself and pushed on, keeping his head down. He paused and looked upstream. He heard what sounded like a hundred wild horses racing towards him, getting closer and closer. He turned to run, and slipped. Torrents of water were rushing around the bend in the river below, and in an instant, in one surge, the water shot up over the riverbanks.

Casey scrambled to his feet, immediately he knew it was too late to make any difference. He reached for the rope as a tidal wave of debris slammed into him. The bridge was torn away from the posts and dragged down into the murky water. Casey held on as he sank into the river.

Underwater, he struggled out of the harness of his school backpack and felt himself being dragged down because of his sodden blazer. He slipped his right arm out of it and then his left, and let the deadly soaked garment sink to the bottom. He breeched the water's surface and inhaled air. He used his hands to search for something — anything — and felt the velvet moss of a plank from the bridge. The current was relentlessly pulling at his body, dragging him downstream. He dug his fingers into the wooden plank as it sailed past him, but he couldn't get a firm grip. He slipped, and felt his fingernails snap back. He let go, screaming in pain, slipping further into the swirling water. The river was moving around and under his body, pulling at his legs, and the debris felt like the sharp claws of a giant lizard. "*Help!*" Casey screamed.

But nobody was there to hear. Bolts of lightning were splitting the sky, and the undertow was dragging him down. He slapped the water's surface, searching for something, anything, to hold and keep him buoyant. The flood continued violently surging down from the mountain.

Suddenly, he felt his hand brushing against a passing branch that was tangled up with rope and rungs from the bridge. He threw his arm over it and clutched on to it.

The hail returned and smacked painfully into the back of his hands. He lost his grip, the branch floated out of his reach. Casey was pulled under. He was exhausted but continued struggling up to the surface...

He thought he glimpsed a kid on the other side of the river watching him, and screamed, *"Help! Help me!"* Spotting the long thick branch of an old tree coming his way, Casey fumbled for it, used it to pull himself up, and felt hope. He searched for the kid but no one was there.

A piece of rope that was tangled around the branch and parts of the footbridge suddenly went taut, snapped, and whipped up into Casey's face, slicing open his right cheek. He let go of the branch, in surprise and exhaustion. Blood poured from his gash, but it was instantly diluted by the rain.

He used his foot to search for leverage below, and felt a rock. His foot slid on the moss, but then he managed to push himself up. He pushed again, using both feet, and lunged at the branch. Reaching for the rope, his foot slipped. His head went under, and his leg became tightly wedged between two rocks. Casey saw the light from above disappear, his heart raced as he endured the river's claws moving around his leg and latching on to his knee. He wrestled with his leg in an attempt to free his wedged foot. The rain-fueled water was getting deeper and deeper. He kept his eyes focused on the surface and struggled to escape. The light had disappeared completely; he was surrounded by darkness. *It's not fair!*

he thought as he struggled. *This was supposed to be a good day! This isn't supposed to happen! It's the first day of summer, the last day of school, the best day of the year! It's my birthday damn it! This is bullshit! I'm in control of my reality! Whose crappy idea is this? Or maybe I'm supposed to die today! Righteous people come into the world and leave the world on their birthday, don't they? The stars were all lined up last night in the shape of the Star of David — it was all over the media — I can't die today, I'm not righteous!*

The desire to open his mouth and draw in a breath was overwhelming, and his lungs ached badly. *It's just not fair!* he thought. He was feeling like the comic book hero who never gets the girl because the two of them are from different worlds. *Why, damn it?* he screamed in his head.

The water seemed to rise even higher; the rock had a firm grip around his leg. He stretched his arms up in one last, desperate attempt to grapple at the water around him as if it would suddenly allow him purchase. He felt his lungs fill with unbearable pain, the pressure of the water crushing his ribs as if he were being tormented by not one, but a legion of underwater phantoms. He yelled at the darkness, *Enough! I will not ... die ... today!*

In a heartbeat, the hail stopped, the river went silent, he felt his chest start convulsing, and darkness slithered in. *There's no peace in drowning!*

Feeling an explosion of light deep within himself, he pushed away the darkness and let go.

THE ROAD WAS NOW COVERED with hailstones that looked like shiny marbles. Terry was anxious to get home to his wife, Amy. He rolled down the car window and stared out at the dark cloud that was hovering, tormenting the town. He wound the window back up, nervously gripped the steering wheel, and pulled out from the safety of the trees back on to the road. He heard the tyres crunch and slide over the ice, and he chanted, "Don't speed! Don't speed! It's okay! She's okay!" He used his left hand to wipe the windscreen, and continued carefully towards home.

The river had flooded and the road was nowhere in sight, he slowed to a stop. He prayed the bridge was in one piece underneath, and entered the flowing water. *Two weeks ago,* he thought, *the rivers and streams were barely a trickle — not even enough to quench a bird!*

Terry put his foot steady on the gas and kept the car crawling across the bridge. The water started seeping in between the door seals and pooling at his feet, he was afraid the motor would flood and stall.

Two-thirds of the way across, he spied a funnel of air dropping from the sky and spiraling out of control. "Oh, my God!" he murmured.

He accelerated out of the water, not taking his eyes off the swaying funnel, which was moving backwards and forwards gathering speed, propelling itself towards the town. *I'm not gonna make it!* he thought as he saw the funnel grow larger. He was well aware that disasters were occurring throughout the world, having vigilantly listened to the reports over the radio. *No local warnings — nothing!* he thought. Mesmerized, he watched a rooftop bouncing around in the wind, like a kite. The sky was filled with debris. The black clouds released their fury as another twister formed and started colliding with the first, creating one massive storm cell. Terry couldn't see the town any more.

The trees arching over the road were unable to withstand the force and like dead weeds were uprooted and yanked into the sky. *Coastal towns are the only places that get freak storms!*

Up ahead, something was lying on the road. He squinted, and frantically wiped the windscreen just in time to see a tree falling across the road. He planted his foot on the brake, the car screeched and spun out of control. He choked the steering wheel, terrified. The car jackknifed, Terry's head violently hit the steering wheel and the car crashed into the enormous oak...

Silence filled the car, and he slowly opened his eyes and took in his surroundings. He saw the back-left passenger door was crushed inward, and could feel the back wheel was elevated. He opened his door and tumbled out, the wind had subsided but it was still sharp and cold on his face.

He climbed over the horizontal tree trunk, opened the car boot and searched around for his emergency warning triangle, raincoat and first-aid kit. When he climbed back over the branches, he slipped, and the triangle blew away. He pulled his jacket tight around himself, kept his head down to protect his eyes, and walked to the crest of the road, occasionally looking up, searching.

Finally, he spotted something further up the road. Terry picked up his pace — the closer he got, the more he could see it looked like a body. "Hey!" he yelled. "You okay? Hello!" He didn't think whoever it was would hear him over the sounds of the howling wind as it increased in velocity. The trees started bending and snapping. He tried to run, forcing his way through the wind; he could manage no more than a slow jog. "Hey, can you hear me?" he shouted as he approached the body.

No answer. Child-sized, face down and lifeless.

He knelt beside the body, gently squeezed the shoulders, put his hand on the back, and waited to feel it rise.

Nothing.

He rolled the body on its side, and saw it was a boy. He opened the boy's mouth, and murky water escaped from it. Protecting his neck, he carefully turned the boy on to his back and checked his breathing. His other injuries were evident: a gash down his right cheek, which would warrant at least half a dozen stitches, and blood all over his left leg. Terry could feel neither a breath nor a pulse. He decided to fold his fingers together and press down on to the adolescent boy's chest, to perform CPR, but it was nothing like the rubber mannequins he'd practiced on — this real body was very fragile. Rain dripped from Terry's hair on to the boy's face, and he blinked madly to see.

No response.

"Come on, damn it!" he shouted at the body. "Come on!" He kept pumping the boy's chest: "One! Two! Three! Four!"

After what seemed like an eternity, the boy started coughing and vomiting water.

Terry quickly turned him on his right side, telling

him, "That's it, good! Bring it all up!" He rubbed the boy's back and continued reassuring him until he'd stopped vomiting the oceans of water he seemed to have inhaled. "My name's Terry," he told him. "You're okay now."

The wind was getting stronger and the storm was back, building. He knew he had to get them out of there. He saw the kid's fingernails had been snapped back and the flesh underneath was exposed.

The rain stopped, and the storm became eerily quiet.

"What happened?" he asked the boy, hoping he'd hear. "Storm caught you by surprise aye? — I think the whole town's been caught out! I've never known any twister, or a storm, like it in this neck of the woods — what about you? You're okay, pal!"

The boy struggled to sit up.

"Take it easy," Terry said.

"My head hurts!" The boy announced as he tried to sit up. "The footbridge collapsed! My chest hurts! How'd you pull me from the river?" He looked at his fingers, clenched his teeth, and tried to push one of his fingernails back into place. He bent his knee and winced when he felt his torn school pants caught on his open wound.

He's hurting badly! Terry thought. "The river?" he queried. "No, I didn't pull you from the river — you're in the middle of the road, about three hundred yards from the river. I was driving. I couldn't see. Just before a tree fell in front of me, I thought I saw something on the road. I swerved to miss the tree, and the car slid out of control."

The boy stopped trying to push his fingernail back to its rightful place, and stared into Terry's eyes as if he were searching for answers but failing.

"If it hadn't fallen ..." Terry began. "That tree saved your life. I would've run over you. Someone's looking out for you, buddy — you're one hell of a lucky dude!"

The boy sat up, leant against Terry's knees. "How'd I get here, then?" he looked towards the violent river, and mumbled, "It was the light – I chose not to die – it was my choice. I did this. Did you see anybody else, another boy?"

Terry watched as the child turned his head towards the river.

"I have to — I have to get home! My mom — she — she's alone!"

"Okay," Terry said, "let's get you up. Do you think you can put any weight on that leg?"

The boy looked down at his left knee, tried to straighten it out, and replied, "Maybe — I think it's just a bit mangled."

"'Mangled', huh? Is *that* what you'd call it?" Terry said. He put his right arm under him and helped him to his feet, concerned because the boy could only stand on one leg and looked like he was going to pass out any second. "I'm gonna have to pick you up, buddy," he announced. "You cool with that?" He waited for him to register the comment.

But the boy didn't move.

"What's your name?" he asked him, feeling the rain getting harder and stinging his face as if it were tiny, sharp needles. He was now chilled to the bone. He quickly bent and scooped up the boy, just in time, as the poor fella passed out and slumped over Terry's right shoulder.

He's so heavy! he thought. *What was I thinking? This guy has to be about ninety pounds!* Bearing the boy's dead weight, he rushed back to the car, desperate to find his wife and get the boy to hospital. Each step was a struggle not to topple over as the wind pushed him from behind.

Exhausted, he sat the boy on the front passenger seat and reclined it until the boy was fully lying down. He feverishly wiped the windshield, breathing heavily as a sense of something terribly wrong came over him. He placed his right hand on the ignition, paused, and addressed the car as if it were a horse: "Okay, boy. We're gonna get one shot! You're an all-wheel drive, and we've gotta jump this tree to get out of this mess! You can do it!" He patted the dashboard and turned the key.

The car came to life.

"Good!" he exclaimed. "Good start!" He held the handbrake lever, ready to release it, and stomped down on the accelerator.

The car tried to pull away.

He released the lever.

The car hurled itself over the tree trunk on to the road, and stopped.

Amazed, he sat idling for a few seconds and then checked his passenger. Thunder clapped overhead, and he jumped. Lightning split across the blackened sky — a rip in the fabric of the universe — and he felt fear creep over his body.

∾

ENTERING THE TOWN, Terry slowed the car to a crawl. He found the main street blocked and some of the buildings demolished, whereas others were untouched. Cars lay under fallen trees. Like a toothpick, a telegraph pole had snapped and was leaning, broken over the road. A frenzy of broken wires jittered across the lanes, raised up like cobras, discharging electrical sparks; Terry mounted the gutter and then swerved back to the road to avoid them. The boy he had in the passenger seat was a rag doll bouncing around.

Terry saw a few people appear along the streets. An elderly couple were weeping over a pile of rubble. He was spooked, his mouth was dry and the blood rushed around his head. He felt his heart pounding, and began to truly fear for his wife, Amy's safety. He picked up his phone, no signal. He checked the boy.

He was still breathing.

He cautiously drove on, easing the car forward over the rubble, and finally turned east towards the hospital. Leaves and twigs were caught up under the windshield wipers and were scratching against the window. He strained to see beyond them as he checked down each road to determine the safest route. The town's north-west side seemed to have taken the biggest blow, and the damage was less as he approached the hospital. "Thank God it's still standing!" he muttered. He pulled on the handbrake and jumped out of the car.

Hundreds of people, dazed and injured, were walking towards the hospital's entrance. Terry carefully picked up the boy and moved amongst the crowd as quickly as possible to the entrance. He stopped at the doorway to

Emergency and looked over the sea of wounded, searching for help. He wove through the mayhem, pushing towards the front, and repeated, "Excuse me! Excuse me! I have an unconscious child! Somebody help me."

The triage nurse behind the glass window opened the side door for the next patient.

Terry slid through.

She gave him a scolding look, but checked the boy's pupils, then pulled open a curtain and said, "Lay him on that bed. What's his name?" She flashed a light in the boy's eyes, checked his pulse, and patted him down.

"I don't know," Terry answered. "I found him on the road. He wasn't breathing. I gave him CPR. He vomited water."

"Has he been in a car accident?" the nurse asked him as she placed a plastic collar around the boy's neck.

"No," Terry replied. "Well — I don't know. He was just lying in the middle of the road. I didn't see any cars."

She looked up at Terry and announced, "He'll need some stitches, at least. We'll need to check him for spinal injuries and X-ray his lungs." She pulled the stethoscope out of her ears and left them dangling around her neck. "I'll find a doctor. You'll need to stay with him. We're understaffed; relief is coming, but I need you to stay with him for now. What's your name?"

"Terry," he answered.

"Can you stay with him, Terry?" she asked.

"Okay," he replied, "but my wife ... I don't know where my wife is."

"I'm sure just as you helped this young man, someone

will help your wife," the nurse assured him, and dashed out of the cubicle.

The hospital smelt and tasted like a construction site, Terry thought. He crouched down so his face was next to the boy's head, and whispered to him, "Just in case you can hear, we're in the hospital — you'll be alright." He looked at the woman lying unconscious in the bed next to the boy's. Her face and neck were blackened with bruises and her hair and clothes were caked with dirt. He thought she looked as if she'd been excavated. She had an IV line inserted in her left arm. One of the two attending nurses jabbed a needle into a narrow, orange-colored rubber tip and injected a clear fluid into the arm. The woman reacted in seconds and opened her eyes wide. She gasped for air, seized her stomach and twisted in pain, and the nurse gave her another injection into the rubber tube. The woman calmed slightly and started taking hurried shallow breaths.

That one must've been morphine, Terry guessed, watching as the attending doctor unemotionally scribbled notes on his clipboard and then hurried away to his next patient, leaving the woman in the care of two young nurses, who were now holding her right hand and speaking clearly to her to explain where she was and what had happened: "There was a storm, and you were found pinned under a cement slab. You're now safe in the hospital. Your injuries are critical. Do you understand?"

The woman made the smallest attempt to nod.

"Is there anyone you'd like us to try to get hold of?" one of the nurses asked.

The woman struggled to breathe and to speak: "My ... son. Where's ... my son?"

The other nurse held a syringe in the air, again grabbed the little rubber stopper, and injected the swirling, clear liquid into the woman.

"What's your son's number?" the other nurse asked the woman, to distract her from the pain she was feeling.

The woman made a choking sound.

Terry's heart went out to her.

She gave a cough, and blood sprayed into the oxygen mask. She moaned.

Terry saw tears fall from the corner of her left eye.

She turned her head slightly and whispered, "My son." She coughed again, and this time, more than a spray of blood was visible.

The nurse let go of her hand, moved the mask, and wiped her mouth.

The woman slightly lifted her arm, reached out to Terry, and said to him, "My son."

Terry's eyes met hers. He smiled as the nurse busied herself by placing a new oxygen mask over the patient's face, causing muffling of the words the woman was uttering: "Cay ... Casey ... my son ..." Before she slipped away, she locked eyes with Terry.

He felt a strange connection with her.

The nurses moved quickly, and the machines beeped and pinged loudly around them ... but there was nothing they could do.

Terry felt conflicted in his heart. He wanted to turn away from the misery in her eyes.

However, he held her gaze while she was dying.

He felt her fighting the pain, not knowing where her child was. *A heavy burden to die with,* he thought.

She clutched on to her last moments of life.

He believed her thoughts were only for her son. Her eyes emptied.

He turned away from the dying woman's final moment.

The triage nurse returned with a doctor, who immediately went to work examining the boy.

"What did you say his name was?" the nurse asked Terry.

Terry pulled his eyes away from the dead woman's, and replied, "I didn't — he never told me." He looked back at the dead woman, and said, "But, it might be … Casey. I think that might've been his mother."

The nurse followed his gaze towards the deceased woman, and closed the curtain.

The doctor turned, lowered his glasses, rubbed his tired eyes, looked at Terry, and said to him, "Why don't you get yourself a cup of coffee while we run some tests and stitch up his cheek and knee? His vitals are good; he's stable. You saved his life. He won't wake for a little while. Go and get yourself some air."

Terry rubbed the back of his neck, stared down at the springy blue-vinyl floor, thought of his wife, and prayed she was alright. Realizing he needed to try to call her again, he said to the doctor and nurses, "I'll be back in ten." He headed out of the emergency ward and came out into the ambulance bay to search for mobile-phone reception. He dialed the number, and when he heard her phone start ringing, he felt joy entwined with fear leap into his throat.

An ambulance pulled into the bay, and the sound of it drowned out the sound of the ring tone.

Terry shoved his right middle finger into his ear.

The medics jumped out of the van, opened the back door, and pulled out the gurney.

The phone stopped ringing.

The medics unfolded the gurney's wheels, secured them on the ground, clicked them into place, and asked him, "Sir! Sir! Step aside!"

Terry moved and the signal was lost. Frustrated, he wanted to scream. He was scared, hungry and cold. He stared at the gurney and then at the patient, thinking to himself, *So much pain and suffering!* He saw the person lying on the gurney was mapped with bruises similar to the dead woman's, and presumed she must have been dug out of the rubble as well. He stared at the unconscious face, and held his breath. Shocked and paralyzed, he forced himself to look closer at the bloody fingers and the black and blue arms. *She must've tried to claw her way out!* He started crying. Her long, strawberry-blonde hair was hanging lifeless, caked with blood and muck. The tube she had down her throat was taped to her cheeks and covering her face ... But he knew that face. He took her hand, and without looking up at the medics, asked them, "She's okay, yeah?" Tears trailed down his cheeks as he choked back the pain and uttered, "This is my wife. Tell me she's okay — please ..."

"Sir, are you sure this is your wife?" one of the medics asked him.

"Yes."

"You've got great timing," the medic remarked. "The big fella upstairs, he knows what he's doing at times like these — I wish he'd let us in on some of his secrets."

The other medic continued wheeling the patient into the hospital.

The other one said to him, "What's your wife's name? Sir, come with us. What's your name?"

"Terry," he replied as the automatic doors opened in front of them.

"What's your wife's name, Terry?" the medic asked him again.

"Amy," Terry answered, following the gurney and listening to the medical jargon as the medics gave the triage nurse his wife's details: "Woman; mid-thirties; pulled from rubble of house; unresponsive to sound or touch; possible fractured skull; bleeding from the head, temporal area; treated for suspected spinal injury; protruding broken left ulna and radius; lacerations to the left side of the head."

"Put her over there — number eight," the nurse instructed them.

They came to a stop, and parked her where the dead woman had been.

The ER nurse pulled the curtain behind them, blocking his view of his wife.

He caught a glance of the organized chaos as another nurse emerged holding a folder and clicking a pen.

"Terry, is it?" she asked him.

"Yes," he replied. "How is she?"

"The doctors are examining her," the nurse answered.

"I have a few questions you need to answer so we can treat her properly. Can you tell me whether there are any serious medical problems — heart? Diabetes? Epilepsy? High blood pressure?"

He answered the questions as the nurse ticked the relevant boxes and then handed him the completed consent form. He took the clipboard and signed the form.

No sooner had the doctor flung the curtain back than the bed's synthetic wheels silently moved down the corridor on the blue vinyl floor. The medics rushed Amy away, and an orderly returned the young fella to the room.

Terry saw the boy's cheek had been stitched up, and he had been changed into a white hospital gown, but he was still unconscious.

The nurse came back, and as she clicked the bed's wheel locks into place, she informed Terry that Amy was going into surgery, adding, "As soon as I know anything, I'll let you know."

Hours passed, and when Amy was finally returned, she had bandages around her head and a cast on her arm.

The same doctor who'd treated the boy said to Terry, "She has a small fracture of the temporal bone. We'll have to wait for her to regain consciousness before we can make a complete assessment. She should make a full recovery. However, the next seventy-two hours are crucial for both of these patients." He closed the curtain behind him, blocking out the chaos.

Terry sat silently in the grey plastic chair between the two, who remained deaf to the mayhem around them. He didn't know the boy, but vowed he'd look after him until his parents had been located. Resting his eyes and praying for the two patients to wake, he hoped the boy's name wasn't Casey.

The orderly came back in and placed a pink plastic bag of clothes on each of the beds. "The nurse wanted you to know ... his school shirt had been labelled. His name is Casey."

3

POSSESSION: SOPHIA. SCOTLAND

S ophia sat with Father McDonald in the church as the warm rays of the afternoon sun streamed through the stained-glass windows. She pressed her back hard into the pew, looked upwards and became transfixed as she squinted at the fragments of colored light. Breathing in the familiar smell of beeswax, she had a sense of security and peace.

"Sophia," she heard and then remembered where she was and why. She felt a cloud of depression hang over her. She'd just turned fourteen, and she felt as if she was carrying the weight of the world on her shoulders. She knew that if Father McDonald hadn't seen the angel at her birth, he might well have had her institutionalized by now — or surely sought an exorcism for her. Over the years, he'd grown to accept that angels, good and bad, are among us. Righteous souls, Ibu, spirit guides, from different cultures, with different names, all from the seed of the light, the one light of the universe, just waiting to share, to guide, but never saturate us as the darkness does. Neither Father McDonald nor Mother Catherine had chosen to share Sophia's secret with their fellow clergy, because the fear of being banished and called a heretic was still very real. Sophia was indebted to both of them for the decision they'd made.

She slowly focused her crystal-blue eyes on Father McDonald's weathered face.

"Sophia, are you feeling alright?" he prompted her gently.

"No. Father, last night I dreamed an amazing dream that felt more like a memory, and it was so sad. First I saw Casey again, the boy who drowned. Then I dreamed that deep within the ground was a burning altar in front of a fiery pit. This time, a savage flaming beast appeared. I don't know what I'm supposed to do. The dreams are frightening, they seem so real. Why did God keep me alive? Why didn't I die with my family? I've wished and prayed to die so I could be with them again."

Father McDonald slid along the hardwood pew to sit closer to her. "Sophia, you can't talk like that! There's always a reason; we just don't always know what it is. The light is with you: feel it in your heart, and feel no fear – when the time comes, only certainty can exist. The shadow of doubt will be the world's end."

Sophia contemplated his words before replying. "I also saw, in my dream, that darkness covered the days. A black cloud of evil ascended from the belly of the earth a decade ago. Then, I saw a flash of circulating blood cells; a girl with dark hair, spinning her bracelet, and next to her, an old key. People had become monsters — possessed — and were killing each other at random.

Then, the images changed to a train; like a serpent moving around a mountain. The driver was on his mobile phone, yelling and screaming. All the blood was rushing to his face, and he threw the phone out the window. It was as if I was following the phone, tumbling off the edge of the cliff. Then I was back with the driver who accelerated, the train went faster and faster. It was going too fast for the curves; it derailed, tumbling over the side of the mountain. The engine dragged one carriage after the other. The engine exploded on impact. All because the driver was full of rage! Then, I was on a busy city street, and saw more blackness: evil clouds were swarming around people's heads and bodies, it looked like static noise, eating their auras, their surrounding light. Behind me, I heard a woman say, 'You have little time before the sun suffocates and the moon weeps. The rivers coursing within the soul of man will turn black. Judgement will surpass mercy, the blood of humanity.'"

"Oh, Sophia!"

She stared into his old face and could see he was in pain, searching for answers he didn't have, and she felt a tear escape from the corner of her eye.

"I'm so sorry your dreams are full of horror!" he said. He pulled her into his fragile arms and held her tight. He let go, and used his thumb to wipe her tears away. "What about the others?" he asked her. "Did you see them again?"

"Casey is nearly ready, he is happy with his adopted family. Kevin, he was in my dream," Sophia replied. "I think he too, had seen Casey drowning. Then Kevin vanished too." She involuntarily took in another deep, jagged, emotional breath, "It's time, isn't it?"

"Yes," he answered, "I think it might be time, Sophia. Father Thomas will settle in tomorrow before taking over my position, and we have the fete. We'll be free to leave soon afterwards. Go on the sleepover with your friends. Later in the evening tell Gemma's mom you're not feeling well. I'll come and get you. We'll head off then. We won't be missed until the next day. Pray to see the way, Sophia; God will show you. Try and have a bit of fun tomorrow."

"We have to leave to see the way," Sophia said, and then stared off into the distance, listening, and said, "Someone or something is coming."

THE CORRIDORS WERE SILENT, the nuns were asleep and the quarter-moon was giving no light, but still the old walls were being scaled by the shadows. Mother Catherine lay sleeping on her rickety single bed, which faced an old wooden wardrobe that contained nothing but two habits and a set of drawers. There, in her three-by-three room her rosary lay on a bedside table, on top of her Bible. Her eyelids had no movement behind them, because she didn't have any dreams.

Suddenly, she was sitting upright, wide awake. She reached for her necklace and Bible and clutched them to her chest. Feeling unnerved, frozen, she waited and felt the silence amplifying...

After a few moments, she heard Sophia's scream shattering the night and echoing down the long corridor and into her room. She jumped out of bed, pulled her robe on and ran down to Sophia. *The poor child's nightmares have become more frequent!* she thought.

When she reached for the door handle, the screaming stopped.

Father McDonald was climbing the stairs behind her, panting and moving as fast as his arthritic bones would allow.

Mother Catherine entered the room and registered the prominent smell of sage. She let her right hand fly up to her crucifix. She saw that Sophia's body was suspended above the bed, illuminated with white light. "Oh, God, have mercy upon this child! Shower her with your blessings!" she cried out, frantically rubbing the crucifix between her fingers.

Father McDonald entered the room, out of breath, and declared, "I think He already has." He stepped towards Sophia and spoke to her in a soft voice: "You're in the hands of God, Sophia: don't be afraid." He suddenly grabbed at his chest.

"Father, what's wrong?" Mother Catherine asked.

He ignored her, and his pain. His brow was covered with sweat, and some of it was dripping into his eye. He wiped it aside, and began to read from his leather-covered book: "Bless this child, O Lord ..."

Slowly, Sophia's body started to descend.

Father McDonald knelt beside the bed and continued his prayer.

Mother Catherine joined him.

The light around Sophia began to diminish, and as

she descended peacefully, her body became encircled by a rainbow.

Behind them, the bedroom door swung open and Sister Clare burst into the room, glaring at Father McDonald. "What's going on here?" she exclaimed. "Why is that child screaming?"

Mother Catherine grabbed the interfering young nun by the arm, pulled her into the corridor and whispered to her, "Please keep your voice down! The child is fine. Father McDonald is with her. There's nothing you can do here."

Sister Clare was unconvinced, however, and bellowed, "What's going on? What's he doing to that girl?"

Mother Catherine drew in a slow breath, and told her, "Go back to your room and pray to be released from the bondage of your negative thoughts!"

The young nun stepped closer to Mother Catherine and uttered, "Father Thomas will hear about this!"

Mother Catherine stepped back into the room, told her "Please leave!" and closed the door.

Father McDonald remained by Sophia's bed, kneeling down and speaking in a soothing voice: "See yourself! See the energy, Sophia! Pull it back towards you, and draw in the light — all the way ... that's it! You need to want to be here."

The light swirled into Sophia's stomach; colors mingled and merged, fading and sparkling within each flicker as the light settled inside her.

"Good girl!" Father McDonald said to her. "Well done, Sophia! That's the best control you've ever shown!" His old bones creaked as he stood up. He put his hand in his coat pocket, took out a white handkerchief and used it to mop his brow.

Sophia's cheeks had turned pink, and her long blonde hair was fanned out around her head as if blown there by a sudden gust of wind. She opened her eyes, wiggled her toes and smiled at her favorite nun.

Mother Catherine stepped closer, looked down into the girl's eyes. "How are you feeling?"

"I love you," Sophia responded.

"I love you too, sweetie," Mother Catherine said. "But how are you feeling?"

Sophia smiled and answered, "I feel humbled. My body feels really heavy, but my heart feels light; strong; full of love; vibrant — a cup with an endless flow."

"Sophia —"

"I need to go outside, or at least stand," Sophia interrupted. "I need to connect with the earth, ground myself in reality." She sat up, moved slowly to the edge of the bed, touched the wooden floor, drew in a deep breath and said, "That's better."

The smell of the sage had almost vanished, and the corridors outside the room were silent.

"Mother Catherine," Sophia began, "I'm sorry." She turned her face to the floor, saddened at the memory of her vision. "He won't listen."

"Who?" Mother Catherine asked. "Who won't listen? What child says 'humbled'?" She looked at Father McDonald, inviting him to say something.

He sat next to Sophia on the edge of the bed, his weight causing the old mattress to sink.

Sophia kept her eyes cast down and announced,

"Father, I had another dream. I was watching over Casey when I saw the darkness was gathering power like a storm. It now has many faces, and lives above us, like the clouds. It lives within fear; thrives in a wounded heart, in jealously, greed and rage; drifters in life who don't know where their consciousness sleeps. What does that mean: where their consciousness sleeps?"

"God will be with you always, I have no doubt," Father McDonald replied. "And I, too, am here for you always."

Mother Catherine had backed away so she was almost touching the wall, but she had an overwhelming need to know what Sophia meant. She stepped forward and moved closer to her. She spoke softly, stroked Sophia's hair gently and asked, "Who? Sophia, *who* won't listen? And won't listen to *what*?"

For some reason, Sophia couldn't answer Mother Catherine. She put her hands under her knees and stared at her own feet while swinging them across the floor. She elected to speak to Father McDonald instead, by mumbling, "I know. I'm not afraid for me, but I am afraid for you and Mother Catherine, and everyone else, because I can see, and I don't want to!" She swiftly reached for the comfort of her mother's medallion, making sure it was still under her nightshirt. Reassured, she let it go.

Mother Catherine let her hand rest atop Sophia's head. "Afraid for me? Why?" She then thought better of asking the question, and added, "No, don't answer that." She felt a chill as she pulled her robe tightly around herself, and brought herself to the present moment. "I'll get some hot chocolate, to help you sleep." She held fast to her crucifix, put aside her troubling thoughts and said, from the heart, "Sophia, have some fun tomorrow! Be a child! 'Humbled', indeed!"

Sophia started to braid her hair and smiled up at her. "You're going to rub poor Jesus right off that necklace of yours!"

THE FRESH MORNING air drifted in to Sophia's room through the open window that overlooked the grounds. The room was the same as Mother Catherine's. Sophia woke to the sounds of hammers clanging, trucks beeping and the hoisting of tents, and soon after opening her eyes she heard a slight tap at her door. "Come in." Her friends Lisa and Gemma burst into the room, jumped on her bed, and started holding hands, bouncing around like little kids excited that today was the day the three girls would be performing their ballet piece in order to raise funds for new computers in the town's library.

Sophia made a quick decision to forget about the restless night she'd had and pushed aside her feeling of impending doom. Today, she'd acknowledge only what came through her five senses and give in to being a fun-seeking teenager. She jumped up on to the old, rustic-style bed and felt it creak and moan under the strain of the girls' combined weight.

"Hey, Sophia," Gemma said to her, jumping off the bed, "I have something for you. My mom bought these jeans, and they're way too big for me I thought you'd like to try them on."

Sophia jumped off the bed and started pulling on the jeans under her nightie – her first pair of denims. She found that they felt strong and heavy.

She looked in the mirror that was mounted behind her bedroom door, seeing behind herself and into her mostly empty wardrobe. She took the brown woven belt hanging off the door, wormed it through the loops of her jeans, and fastened it tight around her waist. She flicked her braid, which was the length of her spine, out of the way and dug her hands into the jeans' front pockets. She liked the new feeling she was experiencing, having almost forgotten what it was like to wear something new.

The jeans were a tad too long and dragged on the floor. Gemma and Lisa laughed as they watched her shuffle across the room.

Reaching the open wardrobe she took out her favorite floral shirt, which Mother Catherine had rescued during a charity drive. While buttoning it up, she became aware it was a little too tight across the chest; her breasts had started to develop. *About time! I hope I get a bit more wear out of this shirt.* She loved flowers and hated the thought of abandoning it. Looking down, her feet were nowhere to be seen; so she decided to fold them up to her calf muscles. She slipped into her runners and put on a sweater because she felt an unexpected chill. "Thanks, Gem — they're great!" she declared, slapping her thighs.

"Come on, let's go!" Lisa begged, holding the bedroom door open.

The three ballerinas raced along the hallway and down the narrow stairs, exited through the kitchen door and arrived on the church lawns. There, they observed the white marquees that were lined up in three rows, piled high with goodies for sale. Cakes, toffees, flowers, hand-made wooden toys and sweet-smelling soaps. The girls wove around the stalls and stopped at the Ferris wheel.

As Mother Catherine strolled among the stalls, she bumped into Gemma's mom. "Good morning, Mother Catherine!" Jillian said to her, pleased to have encountered someone she knew.

"Good morning, dear!" Mother Catherine replied. "What a wonderful day the Lord has provided for our fete!"

"How's the fundraising going this year?" Jillian queried.

Mother Catherine smiled modestly and answered, in a soft voice, "Good. Are you off to watch Gemma in the recital?"

The two started walking side by side, heading for the stage.

"Yes, I am," Jillian replied.

Three young boys who were obviously playing a game of tag came tearing around the blind corner of a stall and barreled into Mother Catherine.

She caught them and embraced them, laughing, and reminded them to be careful.

"I'm afraid this world's going to hell!" Jillian announced.

"Well, *you're* full of good cheer!" Mother Catherine said.

"Sorry," she said, looking at her fingernails, "it's just that it's all getting me down."

"Focus on sharing — and turn your telly off," Mother Catherine advised her. "All we have to do is 'love thy neighbor' and all will be right in the world. We focus on ourselves too much anyway. Was there something I can help you with?"

"Would you mind if Sophia joined the girls for a sleepover tonight? Lisa's mother has given the okay. Gemma would love it if Sophia could come too, if it's okay with you and Father McDonald — you've both raised her as if she was your own."

Mother Catherine stopped walking, looked at her, and replied, "Father McDonald said you mentioned something to him yesterday. It's fine with us."

The two arrived at the stage as the performance was about to begin.

Mother Catherine smiled when she saw that the girls were saying a prayer backstage.

"All the big stars do it," Jillian commented. "Oh, look, Father Thomas is here. He looks so young — well, compared to ... anyway, I'm just going to go and say hello to him."

Mother Catherine smiled, raised her eyebrows and said to her, "Off you go then!" She watched her give Gemma the thumbs-up and saw Gemma turn to her two friends to tell them the good news. *It's so good to see Sophia with a smile on her face,* she thought.

~

SOPHIA FELT WONDERFUL AS SHE, Lisa and Gemma huddled together excited about their beautiful performance. Everyone had applauded loudly over and over again as if they were professional dancers; it was the perfect end to a perfect day.

Gemma snapped a quick selfie, tied her ballet shoes together, flung them around her neck, and with a big smirk on her face, her hand on her hip, exclaimed to Sophie, "Oh, my God, Sophie, did you see that guy smiling at you?" He's a year above us at school, and more mature than any of the nerds my brother hangs with!"

"No. He wasn't looking at me, was he?" Sophia asked her.

"Here he comes!" Gemma said, linking arms with Lisa.

Nervously, Sophia announced, "I'm off. I'm going to pack my bag for tonight... I'll meet you at your mom's car!"

"What, now? No — stay!" Gemma begged her, pushing her towards the unsuspecting teenager.

Sophia pointed her eyes past his handsome face, skirted around him, and ran off to the nuns' dormitory.

"We're a row behind the blue dumpster!" Gemma yelled to her. "See you in ten!"

~

SOPHIA RAN up the back stairs, hearing her steps echo in the empty corridor. She flung her bedroom door open, tossed her ballet shoes on the bed, took off her cardigan, flipped off her sneakers, wriggled out of her leotard, and got back into her new jeans. Full of excitement she rushed to grab a hoodie from the wardrobe, pushing her feet back into her sneakers, she nearly tripped over her own feet as she reached for her backpack, which Mother Catherine seemed to have already filled with goodies. On her tiptoes, she stretched for the sleeping bag that was on top of the wardrobe, she wriggled it off with her fingers. She strapped it to her backpack; ready. She jumped when she heard a series of loud cracks and sharp claps coming from outside. Sophia held her breath, her heart raced as she mentally searched for a picture to put to the sound; she decided to stay away from the window. *It must be just cars backfiring*, she thought. *No, that's not it ... I know! Fireworks. That must be it!* However, it wasn't yet completely dark — twilight was still descending — her colorful happy mental images of firecrackers started to become infiltrated with scenes from the previous night's dream. She ran from the room, eager to see the fireworks and not miss a thing. *Must be the private school boys getting up to mischief!*

Sophia's stomach turned and every atom in her body began to vibrate. The sound of people screaming grew louder. Walking from the direction of the river she saw a pale young man, barefoot, wearing a dirty pair of white jocks and a t-shirt. His long, straight, bleached hair was stuck to his dirty face, his feet were caked with mud, and his black eyes were expressionless. He held a rifle at waist height firing it randomly. Everybody in the vicinity was now running and screaming, seeking shelter. The young man wasn't taking aim at all; he looked dead, and the semi-automatic gun just kept firing.

Trying to block out her own panic she ran behind the church, towards the fete stalls and the car park behind them. Feeling as if her heart was about to rupture Sophia crouched down behind the cake stall, the last stall in the row... *Nearly there!* she thought. She'd have to sprint about fifteen yards across grass, out in the open, to get to the cars. A man carrying his crying child ran past her across the grass towards the carpark. The blue dumpster Gemma said her mother's car was parked behind was clearly visible. Her body felt strange, and she wanted to purge the adrenalin from it. Sophia could feel that her body was changing. Her atoms were now on fire, separating and joining, separating and joining; it was a scintillating feeling. She saw that the edge of her body looked pixelated, and she had to keep herself together, *literally*. She held her aura tightly in her mind, and mentally repeated to herself, *Stay connected! Stay connected! Feel the ground!* She needed to make her legs move. *I can do this.* Before losing total connection to her body, she stood up, staying low and ran out across the open space to the first row of cars. She ducked behind the blue dumpster, then scampered around it to Gemma's mother's car, and stopped. Out in the open, on the dusty gravel, just out of reach, was an abandoned pair of ballet shoes tied casually together. *They look like Gemma's,* she thought, not wanting to move and not wanting to know for sure.

The sound of gunfire was now coming from the car

park, and the sky was turning black. She quickly pressed up against the back of the car and slowly peeked around the car's red tail lights. Between two cars Gemma's mother was lying on the ground, Gemma and Lisa motionless beside her. She edged forward, praying they were alive, and saw that Gemma's mother's hair was matted with blood. She slapped her hand over her mouth, squeezed it tight to stop herself from screaming and moved back behind the car. Sophia pressed her head against the cold metal of the bumper bar and cried, not noticing that the gunfire had stopped.

"Stop! Look at me!" she heard Mother Catherine scream.

Sophia spun around. She was trapped, the gunman was right behind her. Mother Catherine was behind him trying to get his attention. *No, Mother Catherine!* she whispered inside her head, taking a half step towards them. *Please, no! What are you doing? Stop! Please, stop! No! He won't listen!*

Mother Catherine was taken aback by the sound of Sophia's voice inside her head. Never having heard it before, she felt a sense of calm descend on her and a feeling of admiration for God and his creations. *You're an amazing person, Sophia!* she thought. *Can you hear me?*

Yes, I'm here! Sophia thought. *What can I do? What can I do?*

I love you, Sophia! Now, run! Mother Catherine replied.

Mother Catherine, no!

Mother Catherine turned her attention to the young man, and gently said to him, "You're safe. No one's going to hurt you. Please, give me your gun."

Sophia could see he was staring absently, drool hanging from the corners of his mouth. His arms looked heavy, and he swung them clumsily as he held the gun at waist height. *He's going to drop it,* she thought. She could see he was covered with a darkening grey mist that was expanding, contracting, expanding.

Mother Catherine prayed as she stepped closer to the young man. "Protect Sophia," she began, "and forgive this young man, Lord. He knows not what he does."

Mother Catherine, move away! Sophia pleaded.

His black irises locked on the crucifix that Mother Catherine was nervously rubbing ... suddenly, he opened his eyes wide and stretched his mouth in a silent scream. His cheeks were torn apart, and a thousand bees erupted from his mouth. They flew straight at Mother Catherine, swarming around her face.

"Aaah! No! No! No! No! No! Mother Catherine!" Sophia shouted and moved towards her...

... but before she stood up, the young man lifted the gun, and the loud, frenzied buzzing of the bees was drowned out by gunfire.

Sophia saw Mother Catherine fall to the ground, her face and throat swelling up; she was in a state of anaphylactic shock.

Run, Sophia! Run! Mother Catherine mentally commanded her.

"No!" Sophia replied. "I won't leave you!" *Relax! Breathe! Just breathe!* she told herself as the gunman turned to face her. She felt the energy boiling, swirling within the pit of her stomach, and felt her atoms splitting, growing and radiating from every pore in her body.

The bees were everywhere, but none landed on Sophia.

The young man became mesmerized by the swirling vortex of light she had around her.

She began folding and unfolding the energy with her mind in order to create a barrier of space and light between them. She'd never tried doing this before. *This is way too slow!* She saw that his irises and all around his eyes were two black pools of tar, and the heavy mist around him was starting to push out from his being, causing her barrier of light to disintegrate before she could completely manifest it. She saw that the mist was made up of tiny creatures — micro-winged demons — which burst into sparks of light as they collided with her energy. They started flying in and out of the gunman's mouth, nose and grated cheeks. The dark matter was becoming dense: it pushed out violently forcing her backwards. She felt her head jolt back as her body hit the ground, she lost control of her energy, shattering the car windows and knocking the gunman off his feet. Shocked, she pushed up off the ground and crawled to Mother Catherine.

Out of nowhere, she saw Father McDonald appear next to her and grab her right arm. Suddenly he went stiff, as if he'd been tasered, and she could smell the singed hairs on his arms. As soon as he had his body under control, he lifted Sophia to her feet.

They ran down to the river and headed for a stand of trees to hide within.

The gunman was trying to stand up, when from behind, carrying a stone, Father Thomas raised his arms and slammed the stone into the back of the young man's head. Sophia turned away. When she looked back briefly, she saw that Father Thomas was taking the gun from the young man, then checking Mother Catherine, but Sophia knew he was too late: her face was now unrecognizable. She still had her hand clenched around her pendant of Jesus. Father Thomas went back to check the gunman's pulse and lowered his ear to the man's mouth, searching for any signs of life.

The gunman's mouth opened and a dark mist was expelled from it and on to Father Thomas's face.

Father Thomas backed away, coughing and choking. He held his throat as the mist entered his mouth. "We have to go back! We have to help him!" Sophia begged Father McDonald as she watched Father Thomas reach for his head and cradle it in his hands, his face twisted in pain. She reached out with her mind, connected, and heard him begging for the pain to stop — a second of it seemed like a minute, and a minute of it seemed like an hour. *He thinks he's going to die,* she thought as she felt his mind slip into darkness.

Then, as quickly as the pain had started, it stopped. Father Thomas went down on his knees, and vomited.

Sophia saw, from within his eyes, Sister Clare running to his aid and heard the sirens approach from off in the distance with his ears.

Father Thomas spat on the ground, and wiped his mouth.

"Look!" Sister Clare yelled, and pointed towards the forest.

Father Thomas followed her gaze, and saw Sophia and Father McDonald looking straight at them.

It's strange looking at myself through someone else's eyes, she thought and started to separate from Father Thomas.

"We must tell the police about Father McDonald," Sister Clare said to him.

Sophia waited — Father Thomas lost his balance and placed his fingertips on his temples. She merged back completely into his mind, scared, because he was losing consciousness and also losing control of his body. She could feel his distress, his fear, as if he was beside her in the back seat of a car while someone *else* was driving. To her it seemed as if "they" were looking out from behind his eyes together, as if his eyes were now mere windows because he had become a prisoner in his own body.

From deep within Father Thomas, Sophia heard a foreign-sounding roar of laughter, the laughter of a legion. *We're not alone,* she thought, *something else is within him.* She felt a chill ripple across his chest.

Sophia kept her thoughts as still as possible and disconnected from Father Thomas. The last thing she heard, punctuated by all-consuming laughter was, *That's right, priest: you belong to* me *now! How quickly your God abandons you!* Terrified, she wanted to scream, to explode, to get away from the evil. She quickly left him and secured herself within her own mind and body.

Father McDonald pulled her deeper into the forest, and when they came to a small hill, they settled in behind it, on their bellies, feeling like two snipers as they looked back at the church.

Father Thomas was vomiting continuously. He wiped his chin. His body slowly straightened up.

Sophia lay low in the brush, next to Father McDonald, and watched Father Thomas as he waved his fist in the air as if he were a puppet. "What happened to Father Thomas?" she whispered to Father McDonald. "Why did that gunman do that? Oh, Father, Mother Catherine: she's dead!"

"I don't know," Father McDonald replied, "I have a terrible feeling the gunman was looking for you, Sophia."

"Me?" she queried. "Why me? All these people have died because of *me*?!" She started crying uncontrollably. "No," she said, "I don't believe you: why would he want to kill me?"

"Your light. Let's get moving; it's time to leave." He lifted her up by her backpack, drawing on strength she didn't know he still had, and together they moved away from the church and travelled deeper into the woods.

4

KING-HIT: KEVIN. AUSTRALIA

Kevin just wanted them to stop. The sound of his parents quarrelling continued late into the night. Bile rose in his throat as they yelled and screamed at each other. Each selfish word more painful than a slap in the face and the sting of each adjective lingered in his soul. He just wanted them to speak nicely to each other. *Why do they fight?* he wondered. They are both to blame, but his mom the most.

The baby cried. Love cowered in the corner. The screen door slammed. The porch light came on and Kevin moved to the window. His mother stormed down the front path clutching her cardigan. The car door creaked, tyres screeched as she sped away. *What happened? Why didn't she like the gift?* Kevin thought. *Why did she look at his dad like that? What was in the little box his dad had wrapped with care — and what's with the blue tiny esky?* Once or twice a week she left late at night with the tiny icebox and returned in the early hours of the morning, and put it away at the back of the freezer. The first time he saw it was when she had suddenly returned from the States. It contained a cold metal cylinder, locked. At first Kevin had been obsessed with getting it open, but eventually he gave up. It didn't matter anyway. What mattered was the arguing might mean she has the virus.

Earlier that day before his mother went off to work she had woken them with a jab in the rear, giving them all, including his dad, a vaccination. His dad asked, playfully — grossing Kevin out — if he could give her hers, but she said she didn't have enough. They were sworn to secrecy. Together, his little brother, Alex, and his dad cleaned the house from top to bottom, and cooked a mouth-watering dinner for his mom. It was his dad's first day off in ages. Smoke choked the neighborhood so they stayed indoors. Kevin thought his dad was pretty cool and brave, he wished he could tell him. He worked long hours fighting bushfires and saving people — their homes, and animals. That day, the fire in the mountains had been started deliberately. It had been hot and dry, and before lunch it was well over thirty-five degrees. He wanted to bail and go over to Tim's and head for the river, but he didn't want to disappoint his dad so he hung around at home. While Molly napped in her cot, his dad and his brother Alex had enjoyed cleaning the house. They laughed when his dad went sliding and fell on the polished floor while doing a *'Tom Cruise', whoever that was. Someone from the old days*, Kevin thought. Kevin had draped the sheets over the chairs pretending it was a secret club, and allowed Alex to enter with a secret password while his dad made the bed with fresh crisp sheets.

The bathroom smelt like flowers, the candle flames

danced by the window. A hot summer wind came through the front door. By the time his mom came home from work and dropped her keys in the bowl on the side table by the front door next to his dad's, Molly and Alex were fast asleep. Kevin hid under the cool sheets upstairs in his room with his favorite childhood gift, a miner's light his grandfather had given him seven years ago for his eighth birthday, and it still worked. He tilted his head and steadied the light on the pages of his grandfather's collection of old *Sky & Space* magazines. He knew he could look up images online, but it just wasn't the same. It had the best old images of the stars. Kevin believed if he stared long enough at the pictures, when he slept he would dream of being in another universe, somewhere amongst the stars, a place where everything is possible. He now stared out the window and up into the dark sky wondering where his mother was going and why she was so upset. He felt heavy and sad; he didn't understand why he was feeling their emotions so strongly. His dad stood illuminated by the street lamp on the front lawn looking lost watching his mom go. Kevin looked down the street and thought he saw a car parked against the curb pull out. Molly cried. The sound drew his father into action and he turned back towards the house. Kevin ducked and dropped onto his bed. His dad was climbing the stairs to Molly's room. He looked over at Alex — his little brother was sprawled diagonally across his makeshift bed on the floor fast asleep. Kevin lay down in his bed, gazed out the window, listening to his father down the hall trying to sooth Molly back to sleep. His eyes grew heavy, the trees outside swayed and the temperature dropped slightly.

Kevin pulled up the sheet, and began to drift in and out of sleep. He heard his bedroom door squeak open; light and the smell of scented candles floated into his room. Peeking out of one eye he saw his dad's silhouette standing in the doorway. To Kevin his dad looked for a moment as if he was glowing, surrounded by colored lights and he felt an overwhelming urge to hug him, and never let him go. *Why do I see these things?* He didn't understand why he saw colors around people. *One day,* he thought, *one day I will.* Alex stirred as his dad bent and kissed him on the head. He tucked Alex in before doing the same to Kevin. Kevin closed his eyes pretending to sleep, then watched his dad leave the room. He started to cry. He buried his head in the pillow wishing for sleep to take him. Eventually, exhausted just before dawn, he heard his mom come home and the familiar sounds of life returned. The pipes groaned as she turned on the shower. Kevin fell into a deep sleep to a congregation of awakening birds that sounded like an orchestra tuning up as their conductor takes the stage, the sun stretching above the horizon, dawn breaking.

"Body slam!" Alex jumped up and down on Kevin, startling him awake with a knee in his back and a wet finger in his ear.

"Get off me, shithead! For crying out loud, piss off." Kevin pushed his little brother off the bed where his head hit the bedside table. Kevin felt bad and dramatically fell out of bed and faked being hurt. Alex laughed in between sobs. "Sorry, Alex," Kevin said. "But you hurt me, little bro, not cool."

Alex liked it when Kevin called him little bro. "Dad

can't find his keys, can you see them?" Alex said, tapping the side of his head.

Kevin tickled Alex. "You go finish your breakfast, count to twenty and go look in the bowl. I'll be down in a minute."

He watched Alex leave the room and go out into the hallway. He could hear Alex jump down each step as he made his way downstairs to the kitchen.

"Where are my keys, I left them here in the bowl?" he heard his dad, Daniel, say. "Callie ... did you move my keys? I've got to get to work." Then he heard, "Hey, kiddo, I told you not to play with my helmet. What if there was a fire and I had forgotten it? Go put it back. Callie, my keys!"

Kevin heard in his mom's tone that she was getting annoyed. "Why is it taking Kevin so long?" Then she yelled up the stairs. "Kevin, breakfast! Come on, we don't have all day. Holidays or not."

"Where's your brother?" Callie said.

"Where are my keys?" Daniel said.

"Finish feeding Molly and have your coffee, I'll look for your keys," she said.

"I'm late," Daniel said, reaching for his fireman's helmet.

Alex slid off his chair and grabbed the helmet. "Can I carry it to the car for you, Daddy?" Humming, he quickly pushed his feet into his slippers not waiting for an answer, and went and waited by the open front door.

"Daddy, Daddy, your keys, your keys are here!"

Daniel turned towards his son who stood at the end of the hallway next to the side table with the keys held up high. The sun shone through the open door; Alex looked like an angel with tiny dust fairies dancing all around him. He heard Molly giggling in the kitchen while Callie made fun of a boring bowl of oats. "What was I getting so angry about?" he thought shivering. "I've got to shake this monkey."

"You're amazing," Daniel said ruffling his son's hair. "Where'd you find them?"

"In the bowl, where Kevin said. He told me to go downstairs, start eating my cereal and then count to twenty. Then he said I would carry your helmet and find your keys. So I looked and there they were, under Mommy's keys in the bowl!" Alex raised his eyebrows, shrugged his little shoulders and smiled. "How hard did you really look Daddy? Or maybe there are some naughty little angels playing tricks on you too?"

Daniel scooped him up and threw him over his shoulder leaving him dangling by his feet, laughing. Daniel saw out of the corner of his eye that Kevin had come halfway down the stairs and stopped; they shared a secret knowing smile. Kevin was a clever boy.

Callie came out of the kitchen with Molly on her hip. "Oh, she's getting heavy. Here's your lunch. I'm working late. You'll have to pick the kids up from day care and don't be late. Kevin's staying at Tim's tonight."

Daniel lowered Alex to the ground tickling his little feet. He relished the sound of his laughter. "If I'm fighting a fire, and run a little late, I'm sure they will forgive me. What do you think, champ?"

Curled up on the floor in a fetal position protecting himself from being tickled again Alex nodded in agreement. In between bursts of laughter he said, "Miss Bell ... says ... if her house is burning ... she wants you to rescue her, Daddy."

Daniel saw Kevin hadn't moved. The energy in the room quickly thickened and sounds seemed distant. Daniel didn't understand what made it change so quickly. In a controlled angry voice, that seemed like it was coming through layers of glass, Callie said suspiciously, "How do you know, Alex?"

Alex looked up at them both and shrugged. "Did I do something wrong?"

"No, sweetie," Callie said. "I just want to understand why you said that, that's all. Does Miss Bell think her house is going to catch on fire, is that why she said it?"

"No ... I don't think so. When she was brand new, I heard her whispering to Miss Poe when she saw Daddy coming through the gate."

Callie put her hand to her throat with a sigh of relief. "Oh, thank God! I thought you were becoming like your brother. That's the last thing we need right now."

Daniel's eyes widened, and he stepped forward, brushing his lips against her ear and saying in a whisper, "That was cruel; he's standing on the stairs. What are you afraid of? Are you afraid of what he will see? Maybe that's what you should ask yourself. What are you afraid he will see, Callie?" He pulled away. "I don't know what you think any more. I don't have time for this."

KEVIN STEPPED into full view and pushed past them into the kitchen. Before he could escape the tension and pain, his dad dropped a heavy hand on his shoulder and pulled him into a bear hug.

"I love you man, don't you ever forget it."

"I'm sorry, Kevin, that was wrong of me. I can't believe I said that. I haven't been sleeping well," his mom said, reaching out to stroke his cheek.

Kevin pulled away. "Yeah, whatever," he said walking into the kitchen, heading for the refrigerator. Chanting inside his head, *Don't cry, don't cry, it's okay, don't cry.*

Kevin watched his dad through the kitchen window, walking to his truck. Old man Pat across the road was hosing his garden.

"Morning, Pat," his dad shouted. He shouted a little louder.

"Morning, Pat!" "Morning, Daniel. Hear you guys got the upper hand on that bushfire up them mountains. Those eucalyptus trees got so much oil in them they light up like a Christmas tree, don't they."

"They sure do, Pat. Looking after Martha's roses I see."

"Yeah, just as well there aren't any water restrictions. These roses guzzle it up like a thirsty camel. Bring those kids of yours over any time, Daniel, they're always welcome here."

"Thanks, Pat. When is Martha coming home? Soon I hope?"

"Not sure. Her sister has the virus. It's so quiet without her, Daniel. This virus has got me spooked.

When she gets back from her sister's, I'm thinking of hightailing it out of here. Everyone's leaving the city. The crime rate has tripled, all because of a bloody virus. Men, and women, are doing crazy things, violent things. It's frightening."

"Pat, you're welcome to join us for dinner until she gets back, you don't have to be alone."

Kevin watched them, transfixed.

"Kevin! Shut the refrigerator door and go get dressed."

Kevin jumped and spun around; his mom had scared the shit out of him. He closed the refrigerator and followed her to the stairs. On his way he passed the front door. Compelled, he opened it and stepped outside. A crow was circling the sky: *ah, ah, ahhhhhhh.*

"Hey, crow," Kevin said standing on the porch in his black and gold boxers. His dad climbed into the black Dodge four-door utility, and pulled out of the driveway. *It was a beast of a car, two more years and he could drive it,* Kevin thought and remembered when they were at his grandpa's in Queensland; he had ridden in the back while his dad spun the car in circles around the open paddock. Kevin was scared and held on tight to the roll bars, laughing and trying not to slide everywhere. That was nearly a year ago; he missed those days. Kevin came back to the present and saw old man Pat watching him and gave him a wave. Kevin suddenly felt worried about the old guy. Kevin waved again before letting the screen door slam. Kevin shivered, he had felt the warmth of the sun, but now a chill ran up his spine. Confused, he went back outside, stepped on the cool grass, and watched old man Pat, who was looking down the road and drowning Martha's flowers. Pat turned off the hose, stretched his back and tilted his head slowly towards his shoulder as if straining to hear. *Something in the air doesn't feel right,* Kevin thought. Kevin went to give old man Pat another morning salute and turn to the house when a flash of light caught his eye. An unknown car was down the street. *Who's that,* he thought. He knew everyone in his street, and this car didn't belong, but it looked familiar. He raked his memory. *Where before have I seen that car?* Old man Pat was rubbing the back of his neck starring up into the smoke-filled sky. *That's right!* A few nights ago he couldn't sleep and was staring out his window in the early morning, when he saw old man Pat putting his bin out. He had watched him, in his pajamas, shuffling down the driveway, struggling to drag the bin to the curb as quietly as possible. With the bins in position Pat glanced down the street. *Searching for the garbage truck,* Kevin thought. The streets were empty bar one car, which had its front window fogged and cigarette smoke escaping from a narrow crack. It was the same car as the one currently sitting at the end of the street. It had also been there last night, hiding in the dark. Without any lights it had pulled out from the curb after his mother had left, just before Molly had started to cry. Kevin hadn't given it another thought, but here it was, again. He tried to see the number plate; his position was no good. Kevin walked casually to the sidewalk and the car suddenly started up and did a U-turn. Pat looked at Kevin, and Kevin shrugged his shoulders turning back to the house. *Who are they and what are they up to?* Kevin wondered.

Kevin firmly pushed the front door close behind him. "Mom," Kevin shouted up the stairs. "Have you noticed that black car hanging out at the end of the street? And what's wrong with old man Pat? His shadow's got no head."

"What Kevin? I can't hear you. Come upstairs and get ready."

Kevin stood in the bathroom doorway listening to Molly and Alex giggling. His mom was annoyed. The pair of them were hiding behind a cloud of talcum powder. Alex let go of the white plastic bottle of powder. Molly wasn't ready to give up and squeezed and squealed as his mom wrestled with her. Smiling, Kevin leant against the doorframe and watched them play.

"Molly, give it to Mommy, we have to get dressed ... Ta." Through the cloud his mom saw him in the doorway. "What are you doing? Go get ready! We have to go. I am going to be late for work! Be ready and downstairs in five."

"Why bother. Hardly anyone is going to their work with the virus about. I can ride my bike. You don't have to drive me."

She looked at Kevin. "I have important work to complete. No — I'll drive you." She rushed off, dusting the powder out of her hair with Molly dangling off her hip in a cloud of white.

He hesitated and bit his lip, then quickly blurted it out. "Something is wrong with old man Pat. I don't know what, but there's something wrong."

"Kevin, not now, pleeeease. Not now! It's been ages

since you ... well, you know." Their eyes momentarily locked like horns. She pulled her gaze away as if she couldn't look at him another second.

"I know what you're thinking," Kevin said. "I didn't make it up, I saw the boy drown."

"Oh God, not again, why do you lie so much? I thought you were over this. The police found nothing. *Enough.* Go get ready."

He looked down at the bathroom tiles and mumbled, "They couldn't find anything because they were looking in the wrong country."

He saw the shame, the tension in her jaw and the anger in her eyes. Sometimes when he looked into her eyes he didn't know where she was or who was looking at him. Having the police search the creek wasn't his idea. *Why doesn't she listen to me? Please help me, somebody give me back my mom. Why is she so scared?*

"But Mom ... I didn't ... grandma and grandpa ... I didn't ... I'm sorry I didn't know..." Tears started streaming down his face, it was hard to breath, he couldn't speak. *Everything was turning upside down. Why was he even mentioning this stuff; he just wanted to shut up.* Through heaving emotions he tried to hold back each wrenching sob and talk normally, but he couldn't. It was all coming out; it had been a year of holding back the pain. "I don't know why ... I didn't see. What's the point if I can't save my family?"

She stopped getting Molly's clothes out of the drawer. Crossed the room to hold him. "Oh, Kevin, is that what you think. I don't blame you."

He shrugged her off.

"What happened to your grandparents is not your fault. It was a drunk driver. There wasn't anything you could have done. You shouldn't have visions, or feel people's pain; you need to push it away. You need to be normal and have fun and adventures, like all fifteen-year-old boys. You're a good person, Kevin. Look, if you think you can ride over to Tim's without running into any of the infected — well, okay then. What worries me is there have been so many brutal bashings in the area. I'll drop your things off after I have taken Molly and Alex to childcare."

KEVIN LEANT on Tim's dining room table with his elbows on the tablecloth cradling his face in his hands, gazing at his broken image reflecting in the crystal bowl.

"Kev, what are you looking at? Come on, move the stuff. Clear the table. This box is heavy."

Kevin snapped out of his trance and cleared the crystal bowl, books and candles off the table. "Why is it lately when I come over there is a smell of something sweet burning?"

Tim opened the lid. "Mom's been burning incense again. Thinks it will keep the house clean of the virus." He rummaged around emptying out his sister's things. "My model plane is in here somewhere. I know Kath took it."

"Let's go for a swim," Kevin said.

"We can't leave until Kathy's home. She's giving me

ten bucks if we stay put. We're not supposed to be in the house together alone after last time. Mom doesn't want us outside with the infected either." Tim was halfway through Kath's box of collectibles. "Here it is."

"Why, what happened last time?" Kevin was having trouble focusing.

"Don't you remember ... the pool table? Our home-made volcano? Hello! Anybody home?"

Kevin felt anxious, and sadness washed over him. Suddenly, in the pit of his stomach was a sense of urgency, an overwhelming desire to run. He knew enough, however, to know they weren't his feelings and the more he became conscious of that, it was easier to control; each time it happened he recognized it a little quicker. In the past, it had taken him days to realize they weren't his emotions. Sometimes he got lost in the darkness, but when realization dawned, *boom!* It would feel like the warmth of the sun ran through his veins, and he would be filled with excitement, as if he had received a mysterious present. A gift you could lay staring at for hours just wondering what might be inside. Then, an image would start to form in his mind. Just like now. Small, distant, a blur, slowly moving closer, and slowly coming into focus...

Tim punched him in the shoulder. "On ya."

"Piss off, what did you do that for? Sometimes you can be a real asshole," Kevin said rubbing his shoulder.

"Now you're sounding just like her."

"Who?"

"My sister! Man, you're a space cadet today. What's

with you? By the way, have you seen the dude she's dating? He plays third base, big on double plays."

"You mean Nash?" Kevin said, taking Tim's model plane out of its box and sorting through the pieces. "He lives on my street; a couple of doors down. He's alright. You signing up this year?"

"Yeah, you? What's this part?" Tim asked picking a curved rectangular piece of the plane, too small to be a wing.

Kevin took the piece from Tim. Inspected it and handed it back. "It's the aileron, part of the wing. Maybe we might head off to my grandparents' property down the coast for a few weeks. It's been empty since they died in the accident. It would be a good place to get away from the infected until the virus is eradicated." Kevin looked towards the front of the house. *He didn't know if he should say anything. He was sick of hiding,* he thought and blurted out, "I think Kathy's coming."

"Why'd you say that?"

"My mom's dad had a plane and was teaching me how to fly it before—"

"No, not the model plane bit. Why do you think we need to leave, and why do you think Kath is coming home early?"

"I ... just a feeling. She's sad," Kevin said, mostly to himself.

Before Tim could react they heard a key sliding into the lock. "Quick, help me put everything back, or I'll never see that ten bucks."

Kevin grabbed everything, putting it back into the box. "Why, what's wrong?"

"It's *her* box!"

Kevin watched Tim bolt down the hall to the closet and heave the box over his head to slide it onto the top shelf. Kathy stormed into the house seconds later, slamming the door behind her. Kevin froze and held his breath. She walked straight past him, heading in Tim's direction. He was busted for sure. Kath didn't stop. *She always wears gym workout clothes, but she never goes to the gym,* he thought. She had obviously been crying. She passed the walk-in closet, and went upstairs to her room. Tim came out of the closet and looked up the stairs before shrugging his shoulders at Kevin.

"What do you want to do now?"

Kevin ran his finger along the spine of the DVDs on the living room shelves. "Let's watch a movie. What do you feel like? What about —" Sensing something was wrong he turned around. "What's up with you?"

"I hate to say it, but I think you're right," Tim said.

Kevin raised his eyebrows. "About what?"

"She was crying."

They both stared at each uncomfortably. "Perhaps there's something we should do," Kevin said.

Tim turned on the TV and the world news headlines blurted out of the surround sound system. Terrifying images splashed across the LED screen of people running through the streets, others were being attacked by *infected*, while others watched or were looting.

"Turn it off. My mom's here," Kevin said walking to the front door.

"I didn't hear anything. Her car's not—" Before Tim

could finish his sentence they heard her car pull up. The boys walked outside to meet her.

"Hi, boys," Callie said, passing Kevin his sleeping bag and backpack. "I expect you home tomorrow before dark." She kissed Kevin on the brow. "Be careful," she whispered.

"Mom, I have to tell you something. A black car —"

"Kevin, I have to go. I have important work to do. Tell me tomorrow, I'm sure it can wait."

Kevin didn't bother replying. He knew she wouldn't listen to him anyway. All she cared about was her work. Ever since she got back all she cared about was that little canister inside her *little blue esky*.

Her work shoes didn't make a sound on the driveway. "Tim, don't forget your tent. Alex is looking forward to spending some time with you boys, even if you pitch it in the garage." She waved over her head. "Say hi to your mom for me."

Kevin could see Tim busting to say some smart-ass comment. "Don't say anything."

"I'm not even thinking anything. You got a bit of lipstick there on your forehead," Tim said smirking. "Anyhooooo! So who's going to win the World Series? Cough up, how long have you been able to do that?" he said closing the door.

"Do what?"

"Why is it called the World Series, when it's only one country playing? What am I getting for Christmas? Next time, can you give me a bit more of a heads-up rather than a few seconds? Stuff the movie, let's go for a ride."

Kevin watched Tim's mouth move at a hundred miles

an hour. He followed him out back to fetch his bike from the shed. Kevin waited around the side of the house where his sky blue Apollo was. He loved his bike. It was the last good thing that happened before his grandparents' accident. His mom had surprised him with it two days before she went to the USA. Tim came running out of the shed, jumping onto his bike and riding right past Kevin. "Man! Did you just skol a Red Bull or what?" Kevin asked.

KEVIN CLIMBED ON HIS BIKE, coasted down the deserted road catching up to Tim and overtaking. He let go of the handlebars, stretched out his arms and the fog in his head cleared. His ears popped. His mind crystallized. He could focus again. For a few seconds he dared to close his eyes, basking in the light. He felt the warmth, a surge of energy. He chuckled to himself and opened his eyes; *That's what I am,* he thought, *a solar battery.* He raised his fists up into the air, pretending to shoot bolts of light like he'd done when he was seven.

Tim caught up to ride beside him, and shouted. "What the hell are you doing, K? You look like a retard."

"Nothing," he said putting his hands back on the handlebars. Kevin flicked his gear lever and speeding off said, "Look who's the dork now! Catch me if you can!"

Kevin mounted the footpath onto the vacant block. He pedaled through the long yellow grass that slid over his legs, and pedaled even faster along the narrow, dusty path leading through the bush to the river knowing that red-bellied black snakes lay in the scrub, just out of sight. Kevin brought his bike to a sliding stop. Blocking their way was a familiar gigantic bull ant mound. They both knew the first person could ride over it before the ants poured out in frenzy: the second person would become the victim. They stared at each other, then the anthill, both with one foot on the pedal, ready. Tim broke rank first, with Kevin's front wheel inches behind. Kevin sailed over the hill standing up on the pegs. Twisting his body he looked around to see the ants pouring from the top like lava from a volcano. Feeling exhilarated, they kept pedaling, lifting their front wheels up off the ground, riding to the river.

GETTING a handful of brake the back tyre skidded to the side. Kevin dropped his Apollo and ran onto the small sandy patch. *You could hardly call it a beach*, he thought. He kicked off his shoes before racing through the shallows and diving into the clear refreshing water.

They swam up and down the river trying to outdo each other, played stickball at knee-deep until finally, exhausted, they just floated in the cool water. Tim was trying to rattle Kevin's cage. "Did you hear the stories about the shark that came upstream last year? Dogs were taken."

"Shut up, it did not," Kevin said, walking out of the water and plonking himself on the warm sand. "I heard someone say Shaun Grady and his thugs hang out down here."

"It did! And now you're just trying to freak me out, I've never seen him," Tim said, stretching out next to him. "You can ask Spicier. He saw it, he saw the shark." Tim scooped and patted sand to make a pillow mound.

"You make up some really good stories," Kevin said, resting his chin on his arms. "You should write a movie, especially that story about the dunny man remember! Early in the morning, before sunrise, the dunny man would sneak into backyards and collect large buckets full of a family's week's worth of shit, and if the dunny man was lucky, he would make it through a day without spilling any on himself. Tim, seriously, you should write that down. You've got a gift, man," Kevin said, laughing.

"But it's true," Tim said confused. "Ask my grandfather."

Feeling his skin burning, Kevin sat up and went back into the water to cool off. Peacefully, he floated on his back, his hearing muffled by the sloshing of the water rocking in and out of his ears. The silky water and gentle wind eased the heat of the day. Kevin stretched his arms and legs like a starfish and watched the clouds chugging across the sky as he drifted along with the current, losing track of time. He had not gone far when the feeling of the sun burning his face became overwhelming. He dived under and enjoyed the coolness of the deeper water on his face as he swam to the river's edge. He crawled into shallow water where nearly transparent shrimp swam slowly around his wrists. He kept still, resting on his elbows, watching them swim in between his fingers and over his hands.

Suddenly he felt his awareness expand and his senses

heighten as if someone was standing over him, tapping him on the shoulder. He looked up, searching for what was drawing his attention away from the playful shrimp, and spotted Tim climbing up the steep bank on the other side. "Where are you going?" Kevin shouted.

Tim quickly looked over his shoulder, put a finger to his lips and pointed into the bush. He crouched low, slowly moved forward and disappeared. The cicadas' song rose to an irritating crescendo, the kookaburras laughed and the tide crept in. The little beach area was disappearing. Kevin felt sick, something was wrong; his stomach twisted in knots, his ears rang. A cold sweat emerged from every pore. Where the hell has Tim gone?

Kevin waited a few minutes more. The wind blew the scent of the bush in his face and the afternoon shadows started to come alive. All at once he felt cold and alone. "Shit! Where the hell is Tim?" Kevin brushed his fringe out of his eyes and scanned the area again before calling out. "Come on, where are you." His whole body seemed to buzz, vibrating with an intense concern for his friend. The trees were noisy, encouraged by the strengthening winds. He heard every sound, except Tim.

Kevin walked into the choppy water. Tiny waves driven by the wind smacked into his knees. He dropped forward and swam across. Taking fistfuls of reeds he pulled himself up the bank. He crouched low and crept into the bush. The smell of cigarette smoke was prominent. His stomach somersaulted, its contents moved upward and he vomited. His lips tingling, Kevin wiped his mouth with the back of his hand. Up ahead he heard muffled voices. The bush was so dry, with each step twigs snapped as he moved deeper into the bush. A wallaby jumped out from behind a tree and scared the crap out of him. *Something very bad is about to go down.* Still he couldn't see any sign of Tim. The voices became clearer. There were at least two. Stealthlike, Kevin moved even closer and crouched behind a tree to listen.

"You're a retard. I'll teach you to spy on us. Grab him."

Kevin wondered if they, whoever they were, were talking about Tim. Kevin moved closer. He heard a scuffle break out. He still couldn't see anything, but a sense of urgency overcame his fear and he quickly moved forward towards the commotion.

"Hold his hands behind his back, hold him! You morons are wimps, letting this little pussy get the better of you. Hold him still."

Kevin rushed into the clearing and saw Tim spit in some guy's face. The dude pulled back his arm and punched him on the side of the head for it. Tim spun a one- eighty while the guy wiped the spit off his face. Everything seemed to be in slow motion. Tim had his back towards his assailant, facing Kevin. There were three dudes, all around seventeen to nineteen years old. At the top of his lungs, Kevin screamed, "Get off him ..." The thug lifted up his leg and kicked Tim in the back as Kevin ran forward, keeping his eyes on the unlaced runner in Tim's back. Tim's face was red, swollen, and quickly turned from a look of pain into a blank stare; he was a dead weight on a downward journey and hit the ground hard. Kevin sprinted and lunged recklessly at the thug, who mockingly raised his foot again and stomped on Tim's leg ... Kevin heard it snap. He was stunned. From outside his peripheral vision, in mid-stride, a fist collided with the side of his head. Kevin felt himself falling. *What the hell!* he thought. His left ear started to ring and was burning hot. It reminded him of a time when he had picked chilli off his plate and then accidentally rubbed his eye. *What a dumb thing to be thinking of now*. There was nothing he could do to stop himself from hitting the ground, right next to Tim.

It all happened at a snail's pace. He could only watch his assailant laugh and fist-pump the air, looking at his mates for approval, devouring their cheers. *So, there were four, not three,* Kevin thought, two he recognized from school. One was Shaun Grady, the local bully with his dumb sidekick, but he wasn't sure who the other bully was, or the one that had taken him out with the king-hit. He tasted dirt as he lay on the ground. Before his eyes completely shut, he saw an old car seat with half a dozen or so petrol bombs lined up ready to go.

SHAUN LAUGHED as he threw the last petrol bomb into the scrub. He watched in awe as fire raced up the face of a tree. His friends were like statues, mesmerized by his power. *I couldn't give a shit about the retards*, he thought and left them lying unconscious as he crossed the river. Stealing Kevin's Apollo bicycle Shaun pedaled as fast as possible homeward to watch the bush burn from his rooftop. Shaun felt exhilarated, full of bubbling energy. A passing fire truck wailing around the corner nearly took him out.

Shaun dropped Kevin's bike on the lawn, flung off his runners and climbed barefoot up the side drainpipe and onto the roof, dangling his legs over the edge to watch the show. He could see the firemen leap from the trucks, unwinding the hoses. Shaun could feel the wind change; the fire would be driven out of control by the arriving southerly.

5

THE MORNING STAR: JADE. SOUTH CAROLINA, USA

The early morning sun penetrated the heavy drapes. The memory of the warm night clung to Jade as she woke from a restless sleep. She was born in this painted weatherboard bungalow fifteen years ago. She used to love sitting outside on the front veranda during the summer reading a science journal, or people-watching. This year the temperature during the first week of autumn was high, as if it was still the middle of summer. Kicking off the blue sheet she threw her legs over the side of the bed, planting them firmly on the cool wooden floor. She closed her eyes, breathing in the morning, imagining it flowing through her soles and spreading up through her body. Over the last few weeks she had been experimenting, trying to eliminate her anxiety, and it seemed to be working.

A smell of coffee and burnt toast wafted from the kitchen. She reached for her glasses. The house was still. Jade shuffled along the hallway. The open window caught the dust dancing in the sunlight. She lost herself in the moment, twirling past the window; the lace curtain flapped and coiled itself around her. Breaking away from its gentle hold, she entered the deserted kitchen. Two lonely pieces of toast, with a thick layer of butter and speckles of charcoal sat on a plate next to a glass of juice. Jade smiled at the toast, grateful for her dad's effort. She missed her mom every day. It had been nearly a year since her mother's disappearance.

An old Indian man from her great-grandmother's tribe appeared out the front of her home more often than not. Jade could see him now through the window making himself comfortable under the tree, burning herbs in a seashell. Today she planned to escape her personal prison and act like a normal teenager. Today she had agreed to go to the beach with Ben; she hoped he would ask her to tomorrow night's beach party. It would be her first. She crunched on the burnt toast, skolled the juice and breakfast was over.

Closing the bathroom door, she ran her tongue over her just-cleaned teeth, tasting the mint flavor, and blinked a few more times making sure her contacts were in place. Her bedroom was dark and she pulled back the blinds. Her room lacked posters and the general teenage paraphernalia. There was one picture; a childhood painting, an image from her dreams of a green iron gate, with a golden padlock and a beautiful, smooth golden star in the middle of the gate — through its bars, undefined shadows could be seen. Sometimes she felt that the lock was just a lock, and at other times, like now, she felt it beckoning, crying out for her to find the key.

Breaking the magnetic pull of the image, Jade

stretched her arms over her head and removed her night clothes and stepped into her bathers. She pulled on a shirt depicting the structure of an atom and a black pair of cargo shorts. She looked at herself in the mirror and sighed. *Black and black.* Her emo days were gone, but it was still hard for her to adjust. Her mom had said, "Black is only to complement, to reveal the colors in light, and enhance the patterns around you." Jade changed her shorts to a pair of white short shorts she'd never worn before. She padded into her mom's room to pick out one of her colored shirts.

She pushed the sliding door open and the smell of her mother filled her senses. For a few seconds she just stood there. Wiping away tears, she reached in and picked out a rich blue shirt. Jade tied it around her waist, exposing her belly button, feeling semi-naked. Jade grabbed her mother's handmade straw bag, which she had made with her grandmother. Just thinking of her great-grandmother made her smile. It had always been happy days when great-gran was here. People came from miles around to be with her. Everyone was gentle, caring; they called her Great Turtle. She spoke so quietly their ears would strain to catch the pearls of wisdom. Jade thought her great-grandmother had certainly been an old turtle: slow, hard to crack, soft on the inside. To be that little bit closer to her, Jade went to her mother's jewelry box, took out Great Turtle's bracelet and fastened it firmly around her wrist. She ran her fingers gently along the etchings, feeling the notches in the aged copper. Jade stuffed a rolled- up striped towel into the bag and grabbed her hairbrush, smiling at her floating memories.

Her eyes became unfocused as she brushed her long raven hair, thinking of her mother. *How many times I complained about her dragging me back to her work after school to do just one more thing; always, just one more thing.* Now Jade missed hanging around the laboratory.

Her mom had been so excited the last time they were there. The Australian undergraduate, Callie, was packing up, finished for the day. Jade's mom wanted to share her excitement, but all Jade did was pout, being difficult, demanding to go home. She didn't care what her mom was up to. She didn't want to look at specimens of organisms under the microscope, didn't care about the regenerating dying cells. Or the way the deformed structures were transforming: due to one added ingredient, the virus was being destroyed. All Jade was thinking was, *Last year it was bird flu; this year it's a new virus, which has been spreading from East Asia for nearly ten years.* There was always some virus or disaster on the horizon.

"Remember last week?" her mom had said. "You were wearing your great- gran's bracelet when you knocked your drink over and you cut yourself on the glass. You remember that day, right?"

"Whatever ..." Jade remembered saying. Jade had done everything she could to be as normal as possible and to forget how smart she was, but now she felt bad for being so rude. Her mom had just wanted to share.

"Do you want to know what happened?" she had continued, ignoring Jade's frustration.

"Yeah, sure, like I need a bullet in my head." She had turned away, left the lab to wait in the car. She'd listened to music, turning it up until it was blaring and posted senseless messages online. It was well over an hour before Jade had noticed the time. Her mom usually didn't keep her waiting this long; worried, Jade called her cellular phone. It went straight to message bank. *Damn! How dumb is my genius mother, forgetting to turn on her cell.* Reluctantly, Jade had gotten out of the car and went back to the lab. The building was locked. Jade walked around the unusually dark grounds to the main entrance. The compound was deserted. A good-looking security guard, a Native American, lounged behind the desk in the foyer watching television. She had tapped on the glass door; nothing, so she tapped again, he looked up and pretended not to see her. She pulled her hood down and parted her black hair to show her face. The guard's expression changed, his eyes opening wide as he pretended to see her for the first time. They checked the lab and nobody was there. The guard concerned called the police and her dad. To this day her mother has never been found. Jade still hopes one day she will come home.

Jade looked back at herself in her mother's colorful shirt. *Mom would return if she could,* Jade thought. Since the day she went missing Jade has changed, by focusing on her studies and staying out of black clothes as her mom had wanted.

The sound of a car horn brought Jade back to the present. Leaving the memories behind, she quickly caught an image of herself in the mirror. Jade stepped outside, onto the porch and into the embrace of the sun. The old Indian man watched her from under the shade of the tree. Today for some strange reason, it actually gave her comfort to see him. She boldly waved before she jumped into Ben's car and pulled on her seat belt. Ben leant over to kiss her lips, but she only offered her cheek. He was three years older. She looked sixteen and intellectually was way beyond. Graduating junior high at the age of twelve, two years before her peers was annoying; she had once tried to avoid all the attention by being an emo. Over the past year, since her mother's disappearance, she had made lots of changes, from dark withdrawn emo to stunning intel. Girls lined up for Ben's attention, but Jade wasn't one of them, and maybe that's why he found her interesting. They drove down the boulevard to the beach in silence, strongly sensing each other's physical presence.

Ben took her hand as they walked across the soft sand. The beach was filled with smells of suntan lotion, mixed with the hot food of vendors on the boardwalk. The sparkling Atlantic Ocean was the greatest attraction living at Myrtle Beach and kids reckoned that cruising the boulevard was the bomb these days. The water was forever coming closer, swallowing the sandy beach. Stretching out on her towel, Jade dug her toes deep into the cooling sand.

Ben sat on his knees to apply lotion to her back. "No thanks, I can do it," she said, sitting up.

He handed her the lotion. "Did I tell you I got the football scholarship to the University of California?"

Jade, not really listening, lay back on her stomach and twirled her bracelet around her wrist. Touching and tracing the smooth symbols, she went into a trance.

"Let's go for a swim? Jade. Jade, wake up. Have you been smoking weed or what?"

"What, no, I don't want any. I don't do drugs."

"Ha ha, you are a ditz, for an intel. Do you want to go for a swim?"

"Don't call me that. Why do jocks call intellectual people intels? What's wrong with being intellectual?" She could see behind him girls from college coming towards them. Quickly, Jade jumped to her feet. "Sure, that sounds great," she said, brushing off the sand and picking up the snorkeling gear, thrusting it into his chest. "Let's swim out past the last pier of the boardwalk and beyond the breakers."

"Aren't you going to take off your shorts?"

"No." Jade grabbed his hand and pulled him across the heating sand. Together they ran into the ocean, dropping themselves down into the tiny breakers, and molding themselves into the wet sand to pull on their flippers. The waves gently knocked them off-balance, and Ben reached for Jade as the water rushed back out to sea. Suddenly, he jerked away and pulled his hand from her shoulder, shaking it by his side, as if he had touched a fire.

"Did you feel that?" he said.

"Feel what?" Jade looked into his eyes. "What, what's up?" she said feeling self- conscious.

"I just felt a ... zap, an electrical surge from you. I felt a current race through my whole body and I'm standing in friggin water. I feel like I should be glowing right now."

"Very funny, Ben, I bet you say that to all the girls." Jade dived into the next wave and swam out. In the silence under the water she thought, *Why am I with Ben? Am I so insecure?*

"Hey, wait up," he yelled.

Jade could hardly hear him as she dived back under the next set of waves. Beyond the breakers she cleared her snorkel, blowing water like a whale. Treading water she looked back for Ben and saw him still on shore talking to a stunning teenage girl. *Typical*, she thought, and started swimming back towards him, then stopped. She spat out the snorkel mouthpiece and argued aloud with herself: "What am I doing? I don't need this. Yes, I do. I need him to fit in with everyone." She looked around to see if anyone had heard her. She turned away from the shore and began to swim further out into the Atlantic Ocean. Ben finally caught up with her just as she dove under again. She didn't want to talk to him. She felt a sense of peace under the water and stayed there for as long as she could. Her hair floated like seaweed around her. She held it away from her mask. Her flipper dusted clouds of sand off the ocean floor. An old turtle swam below her. Up above in the distance, the surface of the water began to churn. A speedboat was approaching. Oblivious to the boat, Ben floated on the surface, face down watching Jade. Suddenly she turned towards the sky. She surfaced, cleared her snorkel, pulled the bit out of her mouth and yelled at the boat as it passed.

"Why'd you race off?" Ben asked. "And we shouldn't be so far out."

"What? It's not like you were alone for long anyway."

"Jealous are we?"

"No. Not at all."

"Maybe a little?"

"Who's the jerk in the boat?" she said.

"Maybe we should get back. We are really too far out."

"There is this massive, beautiful old turtle down there. Come, I'll show you," Jade said and chomped down on the mouthpiece.

Before she could dive under, Ben tapped her on the shoulder. "Wait. I want to tell you something. I really like you ... you're not like the other girls, you confuse me. You're smarter. You have lovely silky hair, and you have no idea how pretty you are. You have nothing to be jealous about."

"You don't know me," she said and stuffed the snorkel bit back in her mouth.

"I know enough to know I want to get to know you better. I know how old you really are too, and ..." He wanted to tell her he knew about her mother and how hard it must be for her, but he couldn't.

Jade felt exposed, naked. "And what ? What Ben? Why did you bring me here?" *What has gotten into me,* she thought. *Why do I need him to like me so much, why am I so angry?* He started to talk, but she wasn't listening.

"I know what you've been through because my dad was one of the investigators on your mom's case."

Jade couldn't believe what she was hearing. "What?"

"I saw you, at the police station," he said quickly. "Waiting for your dad. I was there sitting next to you in the waiting area. I was getting a lift home from my dad after being in the city."

Even with her flippers on, it was getting harder to tread water as Jade tried to push aside the memories of that day. She had been sitting in the waiting room staring at the floor, listening to the general commotion of the station. The smell of alcohol, vomit and antiseptic came flooding back. She had felt afraid and lost. She had counted anything and everything to keep her mind distracted. The person next to her had offered her a stick of gum.

"You had on a black pullover with a hood and black jeans, and you didn't even look up, when you took the gum, to say thank you," Ben went on. "Your dad came out looking exhausted. He hugged you and your hood fell down and your hair tumbled down your back. When you both turned to leave you looked me in the eye. I felt something. I asked my dad who you were and he said a sad fourteen-year-old girl who Just lost her mother. That's how I know how old you are, you're fifteen. I followed the case on and off over the year. Your mother was a brilliant scientist and you are a chip off the old block. I knew it was you when we first met at school."

Jade was uncomfortable, confused and excited all at once, not really sure how she felt. He said he always liked her, and he felt something special that day. "You knew, all this time?" Blood rushed to every pore and her entire body blushed. She clamped her jaw tight, afraid she would release a neurotic girlish squeal. She said nothing while her body moved up and down with each gentle cresting of water. "What do you think about my mom? I believe she is alive."

Ben looked like he was struggling to stay afloat. "I do too," he said. "Let's go back."

Jade looked at him, trying to work out if he was telling the truth. "Okay, but first let me show you this turtle." She dived under the water.

Jade and Ben smiled at each other behind the masks. Above, the speedboat turned back in their direction and below the turtle swam up towards them. Ben and Jade reached out to the turtle. Petite fish swam to Jade's bracelet and hung on. Ben held her other hand and they both hovered, watching. *He's going to kiss me,* she thought. *How stupid, I've got a snorkel in my mouth.* Jade laughed silently to herself. The moment couldn't last, oxygen was depleting and together they swam up to the surface. Ben was slowing his ascent trying to pull her towards him. She was out of air and had to let go of his hand. She broke the surface and the speedboat struck her from behind. Dazed, she felt a hand reaching down into the water and grabbing her. She could feel her body being dragged beside the boat like shark bait before she was yanked on board. Stars and darkness filled her vision and the last thing she could hear was Ben screaming something in the distance and gunfire over her head.

HER THROAT WAS SORE, her lips were dry. Jade staggered through the mud, climbed over fallen trees, and searched for the sky. Twilight was looming as the sun dropped over some faraway horizon. The trees started spiraling around her. She was out of breath, losing consciousness, falling to the forest floor. *Where am I?* Panic and dread was turning into terror. *Why am I running?* Darkness invaded her consciousness.

She had woken to the smell of the cooling forest, not

knowing where she was. Slowly she got to her feet. Her legs were unstable; as if drugged, she staggered. She reached up and touched her head — it hurt like hell, she felt nauseated, dizzy. Struggling to remember where she had been, she yelled out into the trees. *What the hell is going on!* Scared, she dropped to her knees, her head pounding. Acidic bile scorched her throat and her head felt like it was exploding with each dry-retch. She touched her head and her hair was sticky. She hugged herself, feeling cold. She sat on the mulch and drew her knees up to her chest. *What's my name? Jade. What's my address? North Myrtle Beach. Okay, at least I know who I am! What's the last thing I remember?* Jade rocked back and forth thinking. *Swimming, snorkeling, I was holding Ben's hand, that's right.*

These memories gave her little solace as she looked around at the dense forest surrounding her. *We were following a turtle.* The ocean had been warm and clear; sunlight cut through the crystal water sparkling on the ripples of soft white sandy ocean floor. She looked down at her filthy white shorts and bare feet. Feeling scared, at the same time with a sense of calmness at having regained a little control of her thoughts; the eye of a storm. Jade shivered. All sorts of scenarios were going through her mind. *Where did I get this hoody? Who dressed me; I don't remember getting out of the water let alone getting dressed.*

Jade slowly got to her feet, climbed and stumbled over rocks and up the embankment of the muddy creek. She had to fight off the panic and find a way up above the trees, to see where she was. The light disappeared. Darkness waltzed with the shadows of the trees. A wolf's howl vibrated through her bones.

THE FLOW of life was visible in the sway of the trees. A white deer, a doe, stood tall watching the girl. Listening and hearing the visions of the future. The deer was not the only one who was watching the girl. The forest became silent, the shadows haunting. The deer could feel something, a wolf — its heart was pounding in its chest, and it had woken to the smell of human fear. The deer watched the dark wolf drool in anticipation. It began its descent towards its prey. The deer's heart, beating strong, blossomed with mercy. The smell and sounds of the forest amplified. The girl felt the oncoming charge of the wolf and frantically looked up into the trees, searching for a place to hide. Her shoulders slumped, defeated.

The deer moved gracefully, determined to confront the snarling monster. With each moment her heart filled with certainty. Her desire to protect was stronger than the beast's desire to destroy. It raced towards the girl, watching her, unable to stop her from falling. The girl was paralyzed with fear. The deer saw into the wolf's eyes, they were red, almond-shaped pupils, with black slits swimming in a sea of yellow. It was getting closer. It traveled not alone, but accompanied by dark angels craving to please its master of death and capture more souls. The deer watched as the child confronted the darkness and saw into the eyes of the wolf, into the depths of its soul, as if searching for a sign of hope.

Finding none, the girl threw her head back and screamed as darkness closed in. *Help!* Then whispered as she collapsed onto the forest floor. *Help me.* The white deer, in a flash, came up from behind and stopped directly in front of the girl as fear stole her sight and she slipped into the abyss of uncertainty and darkness.

The forest held its breath, the rivers stood still. The deer's protective aura expanded. Darkness had grown confident from the child's fear. The deer took a step towards the wolf. Clouds above began to shift. The white deer drew wisdom to her side. She had to protect the child to free the future and heal the spirit. The moon spoke, the stars joyously competed to illuminate, and the darkness fractured. The wolf calculated; the pack circled behind. The deer still dared to defy the wolves.

The deer saw the morning star pulse, watching from above and time accelerated. Thirsty spirits and captured souls fed off the starlight. Nourished, strengthened, they rose above the murky tones of darkness and the morning star descended from the heavens. The restless wolves moved from side to side looking over their shoulders and howling.

They became edgy, sensing danger as the morning light shone on them, and the shadows moved with the acceleration of time. Their leader stood firm, growling, huge teeth gleaming. The wolf focused on the deer's veins, bulging with life. The wolf lunged. Like a thunderbolt, a magnetic pulse radiated down. A burst of light from the morning star showered upon the white deer and the girl. The full force of the morning star's energy slammed into the ground, repeling the wolves back into the woods as if gravity vanished along with the darkness.

The starlight dimmed, folded within itself, again and again, getting smaller and smaller, until it became the size of a pebble and floated into the heart of the deer.

Butterflies danced upon the residual beams of light. The forest glowed; fluorescent morning dew dropped onto the undergrowth, and the flow of life continued. The deer lay down beside Jade, protecting her, giving her warmth while she was unconscious. A spark of the morning star light floated from the deer and settled, fading into Jade's old copper bracelet.

6

PROPHECY: CASEY. UTAH USA

T he smell of mounds of old paper files and fresh paint was strong, but the size of the bold little man standing behind the mahogany desk was more captivating. Tiny beads of sweat traveled down the side of his face, and disappeared into the folds of fat that rested on top of his white collar. His breathing was labored, the air conditioner roared like an ascending plane accelerating for take-off. Nevertheless, tiny beads of sweat continued to pop up on the solicitor's head. He picked a handkerchief off his desk and mopped his round head and brow.

"Mr and Mrs Campbell," he said taking his seat. Fat wedged into the sides of the armchair as he wriggled and sank noisily into the leather. "Sorry about the state of my office, we are moving premises. Now, Mrs Campbell, as you know from my email, you have been invited here for the reading of your great-aunt Daisy's will."

Amy and Terry sat listening to the breathless solicitor. He read from sheets of paper that looked delicate held in his big round hands. Amy was torn between calling an ambulance, thinking the man in front of her was going to pass out any second, and trying to absorb the information he was giving her.

"What do you mean my great-aunt left everything to me? I never even met the woman," said Amy. "I didn't even know she existed. Are you sure you have the right people?"

"It is what the will states. The lavish cottage and acreage is worth a touch more than two million pounds, plus everything inside the house and on the property. The entire estate is just less than three million pounds. You may not have known your great- aunt, but it appears she seems to have known you."

"My mother told me very little about her family. She would never speak of them. She said she came from the UK to the States, met my father and they married, and that was all she ever said about her past," said Amy.

"I'm sorry, but you are the only living person from your mother's side of your family. A search was carried out in England, looking for the heirs to her estate. Your great-aunt's daughter perished in a house fire many years ago, along with her husband and their seven daughters." The solicitor sat staring at them trying to catch his breath. "I'll get myself another coffee and leave you two alone for a moment."

Amy watched the solicitor heave himself up out of the chair, pick up his handkerchief and leave the room, closing the door behind him. "Maybe we should go. We have the legal papers for Casey's adoption and his updated passport arrived two months ago," Amy said, examining the office. "There's nothing keeping us here. We've had a rough year. I know the virus has spread to the United Kingdom. Flights have been restricted, but I still think we should do it. We should try and get a flight out of here. It might be safer in a country house in England rather than here in the States. As much as I love the hills, I think we need to do something. The vaccinations don't seem to be working, I'm sure they are no more than placebos. More and more people are becoming infected, Terry. What about that woman in town yesterday? She killed her three children and her neighbor's child, too. Who could kill their own children? Once upon a time people cared, people would have filled the street with flowers of grief, but not today — not any more. I'm scared, I'm worried for Casey. What do you want to do?"

Terry stared into her blue eyes seeing the glow of vitality she felt. "I don't know," he said rubbing his brow. "Let's forget the viral madness for a moment." He leant forward in his seat. "Let's pretend it's not even happening. What would we have done before all this? We certainly could use a vacation. I normally would have to be back at college a week before the students."

"That's if there is any college to come back to," Amy said.

Amy watched as Terry processed his thinking out loud. The concern in his words was like the soft touch of an angel wiping away her unshed tears.

"It's a long way."

"So, what do you think?" she said, breaking his train of thought.

Amy watched as his shoulders went back and he

stuck out his chest. With hands on his hips, assuming an adventurous stance, he said, "Let's do it! If that's what you want, then let's do it. We can visit the cottage, or should I say," raising his index finger in emphasis, "*estate*. And you can decide what you want to do with it. It could be fun."

They sat patiently with their own thoughts, waiting for the solicitor to return. Eventually, he waddled through the door carrying a fresh cup of coffee.

"We'll travel to England in the next couple weeks. Is there any paperwork we need to take care of?" Terry asked.

"Yes, we can take care of that now. I am leaving with my family shortly, so best we do it today." The solicitor pushed papers across the polished desk towards Amy. "You need to sign here — and here. The property is now yours, Mrs Campbell. You can pick up, and sign for the keys from your great-aunt's solicitor in England."

"CASEY ... YOU READY?" Amy yelled from the bedroom.

The rain pounded against the window. Casey glared down the darkened hall towards Amy's voice and jumped as lightning cracked deep into the night and the lights flashed on and off again. "Nearly," he yelled. His words were smothered by the sound of thunder rolling across the roof, shaking the windows and rattling his nerves.

Amy stood in the doorway of Casey's room. He had finished shoving his sneakers into the luggage bag's top mesh compartment and was scanning the room. He seemed focused on something hovering in his peripheral vision. The candle flames flickered in the absent breeze. "What do you see?" she asked.

"I'm not sure. It's an eerie glow that I can't see in the dark, only in the radiance of the moon." Casey shivered feeling rapid flutterings.

"I can't see anything. I think this storm has got us both spooked. Are you done packing?" Amy said, stepping out of the room.

"Pretty much."

Amy left Casey to finish packing and headed downstairs. She lit the candles by the front entrance. Mesmerized by the dancing flames she imagined the rich green fields of England where her mother grew up. She felt a fondness for her home in the hills of Utah and hoped one day she would return. Sheltering the flames with her hands, she said to the candle gently, "Lucky I prepared dinner before the lights went out. You wouldn't be much help."

Her brow tensed and her eyes narrowed as negative thoughts invaded her head. *The roads will be slippery,* she thought. *Terry's not home yet ...* Before she could finish her train of thought the front door opened and a surge of cold wind slapped her face and extinguished the candles, leaving her in darkness. Before she could react, Terry stepped into the house, shaking his hair leaving a pool of rainwater around him. "Terry, you're drenched!" Amy said trying to light the candles again. Then the lights came back on.

"I couldn't find my umbrella," he said, planting a wet kiss on her lips. "Or should I say, *brolly* ... ha ha. It hasn't rained since, well, you know ..."

"Don't you dare move! I'll get you a towel, and help you out of those wet clothes." Amy walked down the hall, opened the linen cupboard and fished out a towel. "The whole house is clean, packed up and we're ready to go." She closed the linen cupboard with her elbow. "I'm not going to have you make a mess. Jeepers, your shirt's sopping wet!"

Terry kicked off his shoes and pants. "I had to stop and help a young fellow and his girlfriend. His car was bogged." Terry fastened the towel around his waist. "Remember when we went parking …"

"Dear, dear me," Amy said with a smirk. "Always the hero, you just can't help yourself."

He pulled her against his hard chest and kissed her deeply. "I love you."

"Terry, do you think our flights will be cancelled?"

"No, they're the last ones. I suppose we will have to get used to this sort of weather in England."

Reluctantly pulling away from his loving embrace, Amy said, "You'd better have a quick shower," and affectionately slapped his backside. "We only have a few hours. We have to load up the car and eat some dinner. Off you go, I'll mop this up." And she slapped him on the backside again. "Hurry up, your dinner's getting cold."

A little later, Amy and Terry finished the last drop of red wine with their last meal in Utah. Together they walked towards the stairs when the power went out for the third time.

CASEY POINTED his torch down the hallway and walked fluidly towards Amy and Terry's voices. He stopped at the top of the stairs and, in a trance-like state and without any emotion, heard himself as if in a distant room say, "It's going to get worse. I've seen into the abyss. The darkness keeps growing. Their fear of the light is diminishing. Only the power of seven can stop it. One will die to save another."

"What the hell," Terry said. "Casey, what did you say?" Terry's stomach felt like a hand had reached deep inside and was shuffling his organs around. He started climbing the stairs. "Casey, are you okay?"

Casey felt himself slowly turn away from the stairs before collapsing.

"Casey." Terry sprinted, stretching out to catch him.

Casey heard himself hit the floor like a bag of cement. Terry was on his knees beside him and held him in his arms. Gently, Terry brushed his curly hair away from his eyes and whispered in his ear. "It's okay. You're okay. Come on, where have you gone. Come on, son. Come back. All the way."

Casey could feel his eyes darting behind the thin veil of skin. He struggled to wake up, then his eyes fluttered and slowly opened. Casey felt dazed and confused. He stared into Terry's eyes for a second, then quickly pulled away and tried to rise.

"Hey, pal, take it easy, you just fainted. Go slow," Terry said.

"Yes. Sure, sorry."

"What do you have to be sorry about? Are you aware of what happened?" Amy asked, helping him stand.

"Your voice, you were asking if I was ready to go."

"That was at least an hour ago, Casey."

"I'm okay, truly. I'm a bit tired, that's all. I'll sleep on the plane."

"Maybe we shouldn't go?" Terry said.

"No!" Casey shouted. "We have to — um — I mean — we all need — look, I'm okay. Hey, let me get the bags in the car while you guys finish getting ready."

"What did you say, Casey? You were saying something before you fainted. Who are the seven? What's going to get worse?"

"I must have been sleepwalking. I think when the light went out I fell asleep while packing." Casey rushed down the stairs, worried they might sense how he really felt. He hoped he hid his feelings better than they did. *It's been nearly a year,* he thought, *and I still can't get used to seeing what people try so hard to hide.*

Casey looked back up at Terry and Amy and watched the faint aura of colors around them change from shades of red to pinks and soft oranges as they accepted his reassurance. They had no idea how much they revealed in a single breath. They were often like the lovesick teenagers he had seen at school. Bending down to pick up the bags, he hid a smile, cleared his throat and looked at Terry. "Hey, don't let me get in the way. I'll get the car packed."

"Cheeky monkey," Terry said, walking down the stairs. He held the front door open for Casey. "The rain has stopped, it's a good time to pack the car. I'll help."

"No, I can do it," Casey said. *He picked up the suitcases thinking, I've stepped upon the path of a very long journey and*

there's no turning back. I'm finally going to see Sophia — in the flesh.

Sometimes she came and protected him at night. She surrounded him with a warm illumination. That's when he felt peaceful, and slept unaware of the negative angels that hung in the air. *Most people can't see the negative angels, the tiny viral demons, but Sophia can.*

Sophia saw them clawing over each other in her dreams, racing up through the earth like starved bats from a dark pit. She saw how people's bodies became infested and how they were encouraged by the tiny demons to be the cause of another's pain and suffering; to destroy themselves and each other. Our inner light is covered with shrouds of darkness until our soul suffocates. We feed them, we nourish them, and they will annihilate us, she had told him. They plagued him with nightmares, images of his mother in pain. Some nights Casey could hear her screams and he was filled with visions of her pleading with him to kill himself and join her. He dreamed Terry and Amy were mauled by black dogs. They would constantly try to brainwash him; showing him that Terry and Amy don't really want him, because he was strange. They would push and push. Casey would wake shaking and feel doubt slither over him. In the day, he would concentrate on others, focus on helping Amy and Terry and anyone that needed help, and the negative angels would back away. The unknown Golden Angel would move closer and in a male voice whisper softly in his ear, reaching out to him until he became emotionally aware. Reassuring about what was right, about mercy, banishing the shadows of doubt. "The tiny shapeshifting beasts know nothing else," the voice said, "but their desire to possess and destroy."

The rain drizzled and the front yard was dark. Casey, torch in his mouth, made his way to the car. He put down a bag, reaching for the door handle, but before he touched the car it beeped into life: the blinkers flashed, the interior light came on and the doors unlocked.

ABOVE THE CLOUDS, the flight to Denver was extremely bumpy. The flight from Denver to New York would be twice as long. Casey watched Terry pale. "You okay, Terry?" he asked.

"Ah, feeling a little sick. I think the first flight knocked me around a bit. It'll pass."

"Here, take my seat," Casey offered. "I know you'll feel heaps better by the time I get back. I need to go to the bathroom and the vacant light just flashed on."

Casey came back and took Terry's seat. He felt the energy instantly from the previous passenger. *An old fella,* he thought, *a fearful, overweight businessman. Left so much toxic negative energy it's surprising Terry didn't barf, A minute longer and he would have. It was like sitting in a pool of quick-sand. First, you're a little uncomfortable and soon you become consumed by it.* Casey closed his eyes, pictured his home and remembered what it was like to be tucked in bed while his mother told him a fairytale. Slowly, the energy in the seat changed. He jolted awake, surprised he had nodded off for a few ticks, but it was worth a mint to have that brief rest. He opened his eyes and peeked at Terry. His color had returned. "Hey, swap back," Casey said.

Amy watched them dance around each other in the small space. Casey climbed over the seat and propped his pillow against the window. She smiled at him and he smiled back. She reached up and turned on her overhead light, and immersed herself in her splendid book.

He closed his eyes and drifted off, leaving Amy sheltered in a warm glow.

He woke as they finally arrived at JFK airport in New York. They disembarked and waited for their last flight to England. Casey felt the red-eye hype of the airport. There was chaos as people tried to buy tickets off those waiting for their connecting flights. Casey, Amy and Terry buzzed around, gazing into the shop windows, eventually settling in the observation lounge. Casey stood at the window, looking out at a strange sight against the beautiful backdrop of fading stars and a runway of lights — the sight of armed soldiers preventing people from running onto the tarmac was foreign.

He could see his and Amy's reflection as if they were standing amongst the stars. He smiled, thinking, *she has a good heart*. She was naturally beautiful; tall, and her long, curly hair was ruffled from the travel, but looked like it had just been styled. *People could think we are related*. His hair was a darker brown, and her curls were more ringlets, but they both had curls. He wasn't as tall, but he'd grown at least ten inches this year and working after school helping the tradies to construct the new Wood-land's playground, and doing a lot of heavy lifting, had filled him out. He thought he looked more like a young man than a boy now.

"Amy, you excited?" Casey asked.

"Yes. A bit nervous. What about you?"

"Me too."

"You know what it reminds me of?" Amy said staring out at the runway. "A moment I had standing in Los Angeles airport years ago. It was so strange. I was a little younger than you at the time. It was the 2nd of September, 10.42 a.m., and we had just arrived home from a holiday on the Great Barrier Reef in Australia. The boarding time on my ticket from Australia had been the 2nd of September at 11.30 a.m. It was an eerie sensation. I had already lived the 2nd of September, it was my past. I stood silent, pressed up against a wall, while my parents waited for the luggage to come around. I watched the people and it seemed like I was standing in a corridor of time, and the world began to unfold in front of me. Sparkles of light everywhere as each tiny electrifying atom of light danced around me, forming clusters, creating different shapes and densities, creating people, chairs and the turnstiles, everything. I felt like I had gone back in time to be in the future. I was from the future. I stepped away from the wall and into the stream of life that was flowing around me." Amy stopped talking and smiled at Casey. "Don't mind me. I'm just babbling."

"Why are so many people scared of flying?" Casey said.

"What?"

"I can see it." Casey watched the dense negative matter moving, growing, feeding off the light force that surrounded people, and their colorful auras were becoming clouded.

"See what?"

"They're afraid. They're afraid they are going to die. Are you?" Casey asked even though he already knew the answer.

Amy looked into Casey's eyes. "No, are you?"

"Sometimes. Do you think my mom was?"

"I don't know," Amy said, not sure where Casey was going with his thoughts. "She would be proud and grateful you lived through the storm. Delighted you can go on with your purpose in life."

"What do you mean, purpose?"

"Everyone has a purpose; we are all here for a reason. I reckon each one of us is a piece of a big puzzle trying to find where we belong. What did you mean before when you said you can see it?"

"Oh — nothing?"

"No, it's not. I see the sideways glances you give. I've seen you take a wide step around nothing as if there was something in your way. I also saw that you held onto that little kid's hoodie. You held him back, just before the car went through the red light. God knows what his mother was thinking, he should have been holding onto the pram at least. You see, I see things too that I don't talk about. But how did you know before it happened. You see something I don't, I know you do. If you ever want to talk, I am a cornfield, all ears." She watched Casey's face as his mind raced with questions he dared not ask. *He's hiding something,* she thought.

"Why aren't you scared of dying?" he asked again.

Tapping on her chest she said, "It might sound lame, but I feel a sense of peace from deep within. Like I have the support of the whole universe guiding, protecting and loving me no matter what happens."

"Not so lame." With the tiniest knowing smile, he said, "I feel like that when I think of my mom. What's the old leather book you're always reading?"

"I really don't know. It's in Aramaic. It was passed down through my family and I was told it was a book of splendor. I feel lighter when I'm sad, I feel found when I'm lost. That's why I carry it. It's my key."

"Key to what?"

"Key to whatever riddle life is sending my way. I don't know why but when I carry the book I feel good and connected."

"Connected to what?"

At that moment, a rich New York accent announced the commencement of boarding over the speakers, drowning out Casey's questions.

"That's us," Amy said.

WITH A CLICK, the overhead luggage was secured. Terry climbed into the window seat and gazed out the small portal at the tarmac. He watched the luggage being tossed on the conveyor belt before it travelled into the belly of the plane.

"Terry!" Amy said.

"Yeah?"

With her eyebrows raised, and a sideways nod of her head, Amy indicated for him to get up and give the seat to Casey. She smiled at Casey as Terry gave a boyish look as if to say, *Do I have to?*

"Getting up," Terry said. "Right — of course, just checking all's well. Casey, my man — your seat."

Casey laughed and said, "Definitely."

The engines roared as the plane sped down the runway. Their heads were pushed back into the seat. Amy held Terry's hand and smiled at him. Casey imagined a giant hand came up from the ground, wrapped around the belly of the plane and propelled them into the electrified sky.

CASEY'S HEAD banged against the window and he woke with a fright. "Turbulence," Amy said, as the plane bounced up and down a little more. Casey rubbed his shoulder as if it was sore. "Are you okay?" Amy asked. Her arm flew up to her head as an overhead locker flung open, and handbags and jackets tumbled out falling on top of her. With her arm she knocked the stuff to the ground. The plane continued to shake violently and dropped, then levelled out. Amy had started counting. "That was the longest drop," she said, with her hand on her chest as if catching her breath. "My heart was in my mouth." She looked at Terry strangling the armrest, his knuckles white.

The air hostesses failed to conceal the worry on their faces, clutching onto their own restraints with both hands as they were jostled in their seats. Beyond Casey, Amy could see black clouds and lightning flashing outside the window.

Adrenalin raced through Amy. Casey appeared calm to her, stillness encompassing him. He reached his hand towards the navigation map on the screen imbedded in the headrest of the seat in front and placed his finger over the image of the plane.

Some people screamed, terrified, as the plane suddenly dropped again. The lights went out. A strong voice came over the intercom asking everyone to stay calm. Amy checked on Casey. He now looked feverish, beads of sweat tracking down his temple. He held his finger firmly against the screen; it was the only screen that still had power. "Sit back, Casey!" she yelled over the noise. Casey kept his finger steady on the tiny image of the plane while chaos went on around him. He was still, as if he was in a bubble, in a different time and space. The plane steadied, the people stopped screaming, and Casey collapsed back into his seat, breathless as a marathon runner, pale and exhausted. His curly mane was soaked. Amy, not sure what she had just witnessed, leant over to him and put her hand on his knee. Heat radiated from his body. "Casey, what's wrong?"

Casey rested his head against the cool window as the plane safely passed the edge of the expanding cloud of dark matter. "I'm alright, just scared, that's all. Can I have some water please, Amy?"

Amy handed him her bottled water and another

bottle to Terry and they both skolled it. Casey retrieved his pillow off the floor, putting it between his head and the window. He closed his eyes and took a deep breath. "I'm okay — just need to sleep for a while. That's all."

Amy leant into Terry, kissed his cheek and whispered in his ear, "We need to drop for a lot longer, before we spin out of control. Count, each time we drop, count. But if we're going to go — enjoy the view. What else can you do?" She smiled at her husband.

The flight attendants moved through the plane offering juice, pillows and blankets and reassuring everyone the turbulence was over. Amy could see the color returning to Terry's cheeks.

Lightning cracked in the distance and Terry turned away from the window back towards Amy in wonderment. "Who are you? Where did you come from? And what did you do with my wife?"

Amy squeezed his hand, closed her eyes and tried to make sense of what just happened, if anything at all. *I am so tired,* she thought. *What did I see?* Lightning flared across the sky. Amy stood up and reached over the boys to pull down the window shade and then tightened up her seat belt. The plane hit a bump again, Terry grabbed her arm and started counting. Lightning lit up the plane once more and the thunder rumbled. The crew closed all the blinds and the plane settled down to the illusion of calm for the rest of the flight.

7

BEYOND REALITY: KEVIN. AUSTRALIA

Kevin slowly opened his eyes and gagged. Everything was blurry. The bush was saturated with the smell of smoke, burnt fur and overcooked meat. The taste and textures latched onto the back of his throat. Kevin's hand flew up to his mouth and nose. In the pit of his stomach, deep in his solar plexus, he felt animals screaming and the trees crying. He saw Tim motionless, his back lobster-red, scorched from the sun. Kevin scanned the area. They were alone.

Kevin looked past Tim, into the bush. It looked different. It was lush, brighter, practically fluorescent, and absent of smoke. Between it and Tim was a shimmering transparent wall. It looked like fluid; it moved rhythmically, rippling like the wind on the surface of a lake, or the vapors on the road on a summer's day. *It must be a mirage*, Kevin thought. He continued to scan the area. He saw the old car seat. *No petrol bombs and no teenagers, so how long has it been?* His skin was just as red as Tim's and felt like it would blister. Kevin awkwardly pushed himself into a sitting position.

"Tim. Tim!" Kevin stopped and stared at Tim's back. He searched for signs of life. Kevin held his breath, waited, afraid to move. There it was. Tim's back rose slightly with a shallow breath, and then another one. Kevin's shoulders dropped as he exhaled. He got to his feet and walked around and looked into Tim's face. He lifted Tim's eyelids — no response. He shook Tim's shoulders and still nothing. The southerly had scattered embers carelessly on both sides of the river; small pockets of fire flared up around them. Kevin heard — mixed with the crackling of the fire — a low hum, a sonic pulse resonating. Kevin turned and the lush green rainforest was still there, distorted behind the rippling wall. It was from this mirage that the sound and energy was emanating. The two landscapes were not quite worlds apart. His world was surrounded by sizzling heat and smelt like death. On the other side of the wall the world looked vibrant, tropical, fresh and rich like a cool volcanic rainforest. *It has to be a mirage*, he thought. His brain was playing tricks, protecting him. A loud crack like a stockman's whip, followed by a soft pulse, reverberated around him, reminding Kevin of a time when his granddad took him to a naval air show and from the deck of a carrier he saw a fighter plane traveling faster than the speed of sound to create a sonic shockwave over the ocean.

The wall was a veil between two worlds. Transparent liquid metal; horizontal ripples plasma-like. Kevin walked over to it. His palm open he reached out and gently touched the surface. Bolts of colored light flared from his hand and expanded along the wall. He pulled back. Arm outstretched he slowly placed his palm on the wall and again bolts of light flared. His hand, the nucleus, glowed. His mouth dropped opened in awe. The fluorescent waves of light ignited by his touch rippled and shimmered across the surface. Kevin felt euphoric — no pain, no fear. It wasn't hot or cold. It had no smell and felt just a little ... like jelly that hadn't quite set. Kevin applied pressure and his hand started to sink into the liquid. Cautiously, he pushed his arm into the wall to the depth of his shoulder and drew in a shocked breath: his sunburnt arm felt cooled instantly. He pushed a little further to penetrate its depths completely. He stopped his fingers now on the other side and he could feel cool air. He wiggled his fingers. It was nothing like the stifling humid air around him. He drew his arm out of the wall. *What the hell?* He stood there, turning his arm over and over to examine the skin. It had lost its lobster-red glow and was pale and fresh, the scorching sunburn had vanished.

Smoke suddenly filled Kevin's lungs and he had a fit of coughing and his eyes stung. The fire was now practically encircling them. Frantically, he searched for a way out, but saw only the rippling wall and its mysterious world.

"Tim, wake up. Wake up, Tim!"

Tim lay motionless, his leg badly twisted. *Crushed more like it.* Kevin searched the ground to find something, anything, to support Tim's leg. Every time he twisted his body his scorched back hurt. He found an old boot.

Feeling inspired he picked up a couple of branches and tore long strips from a paperbark tree. A foreign thought jumped into his mind: *Get out and forget about Tim.* Startled, he fumbled with the boot, dropping it and just missing Tim's head.

Shit! How the hell do I do this? Okay, stop thinking, just do! Kevin dropped to his knees and quickly created a brace by winding the paperback around the two small branches to secure them to his mate's leg. His jaw was clenched tight as he was worried about hurting his friend. Mindful of his own leg starting to throb with pain, Kevin stopped. He was sympathetically feeling Tim's unavoidable pain. He ignored the sweat dripping from his brow. His fringe irritatingly clung to his face; he pushed it back with his forearm and out of his eyes. Kevin drew in a deep breath trying to calm down when a thought of his nanna emerged in his mind and a reassuring sensation enveloped him. Kevin struggled to refocus, blocking out his friend's pain. His own screaming emotions were enough. A flood of compassion, coming from Tim, washed over Kevin. Tim was aware, on some higher level, of Kevin's actions. Kevin's eyes clouded with tears as his friend's emotions embraced him and he had to wipe them away. His hands shaking, he wove a bootlace around Tim's leg brace, adding that extra bit of strength. Kevin checked the firmness of the splint, of each piece of paperbark, and finally of the snaking bootlace securing the bark. Kevin lifted Tim under the arms and dragged him towards the wall, gently placing him beside it.

"I'll go through first," he said to Tim as if he was

conscious, "and make sure it's not going to vaporize us."

The air was getting thin as the fire sucked up the oxygen around them.

Kevin's eyes strained to see through the smoke and the mirage. "What is this stuff?" he said. He hoped Tim would answer. Reluctantly, he raised his right arm and softly laid his palm to the surface once again. It vibrated, light shone magically around his hand and shockwaves of colors extended out across its surface. He placed his left hand upon it and the same thing happened. With both hands poised as if to push open a door Kevin felt the coolness and pushed into it slowly. There was little resistance. He felt his fingers pass beyond the gel-like substance. His hands pierced all the way to the other side, and he clapped. He heard nothing — he did it again, not a hint of sound from the other side. He still felt relaxed, hypnotized by the sparkling lights that increased the deeper he penetrated into the wall, and the humming sound — as if the bass strings of a cello were being plucked — echoed around him. Instantly, Kevin snapped back into reality as Tim coughed. His lips looked red and swollen ... as he tried to speak the sound turned into a terrified wail. It burrowed into the very marrow of Kevin's bones. Tim stopped moving and screaming. He stared up at Kevin, searching with his swollen eyes for answers. Kevin wanted to move away from Tim's pain; instead he stepped forward towards him, took a deep breath when unexpectedly he smelt his nanna's house, lemongrass, and sage. Kevin psychically pushed back Tim's pain and fear.

"Hey, man! Welcome back," Kevin said crouching

next to him. "You're pretty messed up, go slow." The smoke was getting dense, making it harder to see the oncoming flames. There was an eerie thunderous sound, like stampeding horses.

"What happened? Who were those psychos? What a pack of assholes!" Tim said. Each word sounded as if he had been to the dentist and his mouth was full of cotton.

Tim placed his palms flat on the ground determined to sit up. Slowly he began to lift his upper body, cringing in pain as his face twisted into fear seeing his broken leg. "What happened? Blood — what, whose ... I don't like blood especially if it's mine." He started choking, gagging and coughing, causing more pain and he collapsed back onto the ground and passed out.

"Tim? Tim!" Kevin slapped his face. "Tim, wake up, come on, man!"

Tim laid still, his face wet. Tears escaped his closed eyes and he whispered, "We need help. I can't, I can't believe you just bitch-slapped me, K." Tim slowly opened his eyes. "Give me a hand." This time Tim moved very slowly and sat up and stared down at his leg. "Did you do this?" Tim said pointing at the splint. "Thanks, man, thanks. I always thought you had a spark of decency hidden somewhere. I don't know if I would have done the same for you."

"We don't have time for you to get all ... whatever. We're about to be cremated."

Tim, because of the pain in his leg, struggled to move. "What's your plan? Have you seen us getting out of here in one of your visions? Or do you see my mom crying at my funeral?"

"Don't laugh. I think we are at the edge of a parallel universe."

Tim raised his eyebrows and started to grin. He choked on the smoke and said, "You got hit in the head, didn't you?"

"Turn around," Kevin said.

Tim craned his neck around slowly, his skin feeling like it might tear. "No shit. Wow ... what the ... is that a mirage? Maybe we're already dead?"

"I put my arm in," Kevin said, twisting and turning his forearm. "Look at it," he almost shouted, "the sunburn is gone."

Tim, for a second, forgot about his pain. His mouth hung open as he stared at Kevin's arm. "But, how, what is it? We don't know anything about it. We can't just ..." He started coughing, "Your dad will be here soon. Let's just sit here and wait."

"*No! He won't!* He doesn't know we're here. They will protect the houses at the edge of the bush with a fire-break and let this burn itself out." The roar of the fire grew louder and Kevin barely noticed they had started shouting to be heard. "This is our only chance. I can't see any other way, we have to take it!"

Mumbling, Tim looked up towards the sky, pleading to God to save them from the inferno around them.

"What are you doing?" Kevin yelled. "This is our opportunity," and he pointed towards the wall. "We've already got an escape route. Fair dinkum, mate, you're blind sometimes. Let's drag your sorry ass over to the other side and get out of here. What other choices do we have? To stay is to die. This is going to be ... an adventure.

Yeah, an adventure." Sweat glistened over Kevin's youthful body which had a hint of the strong man he could become. Pain shot up Tim's leg as Kevin dragged him head-first into the coolness of the unknown substance. Instantly, they both felt soothed, calm, but Tim's leg was still on the other side and Kevin could feel Tim's pain and the heat of the fire. As each part of Tim's body passed through the invisible wall he felt renewed, he felt his body meld into the rhythm of the wall. Then the pain left, the choking smoke in his lungs cleared. He moved slowly, afraid Tim's pain would return. Fear dissolved before it could completely take over his mind. Kevin and Tim emerged from the wall and into the parallel world.

Kevin stared at what had been his sunburnt chest. They both looked back to where they had come from and watched a tsunami of fire race towards them. They instinctively braced themselves, protectively covered their heads for impact. The flames passed over them without even a warm breath upon them. Safely cocooned within the enclosure, they lowered their arms.

"K, my leg!" Slowly Tim stood up and put weight on his damaged leg. His knee clicked into place. The pain was non-existent, it felt fine. Kevin watched as Tim apprehensively put a little more weight on it, balancing on one leg, then he quickly removed the brace Kevin had crudely constructed. Kevin couldn't believe what he saw; Tim was completely healed. No broken bones, no blood, no sunburn and no swollen face, just dirt and dried blood.

Where are we? Kevin wondered. "We have walked

through the bushes and swum in the river a trillion times and I have never seen this before." Kevin reached out towards a tree and laid his hand slowly upon the glowing trunk. He felt like he was part of it and suddenly felt himself stretch up and into the heavens. His arms stretched out wide, and his feet sank deep into the ground. He withdrew his hand. Being polite, he bowed, as if apologizing for the intrusion. Giving thanks, he stepped back and walked to the next tree. *Maybe we have never seen this because we never needed to be here before?*

"Where're you going? I don't believe this, K. The flames are right there but I can't feel them." Tim looked puzzled, suspicious, and touched the wall, which felt to him like wet jelly.

Kevin bent down into the foliage around him. He felt like he could hear it holding its breath, waiting. He touched the embellished, long drooping leaf next to him very gently. He looked even closer and was dazzled by a translucent blue insect sitting on the velvet leaf.

"What do you think this is? I've never seen anything like it." Its wings were like a cicada's, clear and fragile with fluorescent magenta veins glowing and an ethereal body of flickering silver lights. It was beautiful. Kevin leant forward to coax it onto his hand. It didn't move, so he tried to pick it up, but he couldn't touch it; his fingers tingled as they passed through the creature.

Tim screamed. Kevin's concentration shattered and he swiveled around. Flames licked the wall and a black mass of dark matter had developed, moving in a circular motion, pressing itself against the wall. It moved faster, getting stronger, expanding up the wall threatening to swallow them whole. "What the hell!" Kevin yelled. "What are you doing?"

Tim had pushed his arm through the wall, beyond the safety of their sanctuary. Flames licked at his fingers; they turned black as he screamed. The dark matter took form, latching onto Tim's arm, pulling it out of shape, wrenching at him, trying to pull him through the wall.

Kevin raced over, lunged for his friend and pulled on his other arm. He wasn't strong enough and Tim's arm slipped further into the fire and the dark swirling matter stretched it as if it was rubber, deeper into its vortex. Kevin watched shades of grey shadows flying anticlockwise within the whirlpool's black hole. Petrified and shocked as he was, he couldn't believe Tim hadn't passed out. His arm was covered in bubbling blisters. The heat and pain must have been excruciating.

Tim's face merged into the wall and his screams echoed in Kevin's head. *He's not going to last much longer and I can't hold him*, he thought. *Oh God, where can I get help? What's going on? Shit — Shit — SHIT!* Tim went limp in his arms. Kevin dug his heels in, but he was sliding and his body felt strange, suddenly sick, faint and weak.

Kevin became aware of the tiny blue insect that landed upon his shoulder and moved to the back of his neck. It burrowed into his skin and spread through his body deep to the cellular level. It injected its light into Kevin's atoms, as a bee's stinger might.

Illuminated, Kevin felt empowered and yanked hard on Tim's arm and he tumbled back in towards him. They both went flying. Kevin hit the ground, the wind knocked out of him. He stood and hunched over trying to catch his breath. Kevin felt like he was choking. He coughed and coughed and choked, until a winged ball of blue light shot out from his mouth. It hovered and looked at him before flying away. Kevin watched it disappear into the atmosphere, drew in a deep breath and whispered, "Tim, Tim ..." There was no answer. Kevin was afraid his friend was dead, toasted. He turned Tim over. Shimmering light frantically swam around Tim's body; the light was so bright Kevin had to cover his eyes. He could smell the burnt flesh, and he could hear Tim's arm sizzle, like when his dad tossed beer onto a BBQ to give the sausages that extra flavor. He dare not look. A deafening sonic buzz erupted. Then silence.

"K, Kev, what's wrong with your eyes?"

Kevin held his hands tight against his face, afraid if he let them drop he would see his friend as a ghost, talking to him from beyond.

"K, you're scaring me, show me your face."

Kevin slowly dragged his hands down his face and peeked between his fingers. He saw a hand coming towards him, touching him, trying to pull his hands away from his face. They felt clammy, cool. Not like hands that had just been consumed by flames.

"Look at me, not a mark on me," Tim said turning his arm over. "I feel great! But what the hell was that?"

Kevin looked up and down and all over Tim's body and couldn't find a mark on him. Kevin then turned his attention towards the black mass. "Can you see them?" he said to Tim. "In there, swimming within the vortex, those images, creatures with half faces." Misty bodies reached out as if to grab them, but turned to smoke, sinking down into the vortex like oil swirling in water.

Kevin stared into the darkness and knew that if Tim had been sucked back to the other side it would have consumed him forever. *What the hell?* he thought. *The life force would have been drawn out of us both. Our souls lost forever, trapped.* The whirlpool began to lose its strength and just before it completely disappeared, Kevin thought he saw a claw, the same claw that had reached up out of the murky river and grabbed hold of the curly headed boy. That was a year ago, but it felt like yesterday.

"Earth to Kev, you're babbling again. Where do you keep going, man? Stop this shit. You're scaring me now. I want to go home. I'm hungry," Tim said.

"How can you be hungry? Look around you. This is incredible — look at yourself; you were the pig on the spit. You were nearly sucked into a vortex full of God knows what! How can you be hungry?"

"You'll have to ask my gut. This is too weird for me, Kev. I have memories of my arm burning, but I have no scars. This might be right up your alley. If it's on TV I'm good, but this is real life shit."

"I hear you, man. I don't know if I should be scared or excited, but ..." Kevin's eyes squinted. He looked beyond the shimmering wall. Time had passed and the fire was out. The bush was charcoal and the sun was setting. *It's daylight saving time,* Kevin thought, *so it's got to be after eight in the evening. But how can that be, we have only been in here for ... what?* Kevin's thoughts stopped mid-sentence: *How long has it been.*

All concept of time started to elude him. "Couldn't be

no more than twenty minutes surely," but the poor trees smoldered in the setting sun.

"We should go," Tim said.

"You're right, Tim. Your tummy rumbling is right on the mark, it must be way past dinner. Your sister is probably waiting to kill us. Let's walk towards home from this side, that way. We are safe a little longer, from ..." Kevin was not sure from what or whom, and whether it would be waiting for them, and walked deeper into the forest. Tiny birds of different colors — deep blue, green, red and purple — that were even smaller than finches, flew around them excited to have visitors. The luminous ferns, rich in color, glittered and appeared to be reaching out to gently touch Tim's leg.

"K — I think the plants are alive. Can you feel it?"

Kevin could feel it all right. He could hear them, too — soft harmonious sounds in his head. With each step he felt like he was walking on a sleeping giant and the trees were bowing down as he passed. He thought of a breeze, or the lack of, and then there was a wind rustling through the leaves. Kevin felt like he was a battery, charging up with every passing moment. The sun never seemed to move from directly above them, even though he couldn't actually see it. He could feel the rays shining down on him.

"K, do you think we're ...?"

"What?"

"Dead?" Tim said.

"We can't be."

"This place is strange," Tim commented, as they walked on. "I have lived here all my life and I've never seen it before. This is a rainforest. Our homes are surrounded by bush and everything is mostly dry. We look like we are on our way to Emerald City, and we've just got to find the yellow brick road. It's got to be at least twenty degrees cooler in here. I just had the shit kicked out of me and my arm was burnt to a cinder. My mom says that about Kath's cooking. I sound like my mom! This isn't normal!" Tim said.

Kevin stopped walking. "Don't freak out. Let's go back to the wall and take our chances on the other side. I'm not quite sure of our direction anymore."

"It's more like a membrane than a wall," Tim said, proud of his choice of words.

"A membrane is a wall, but not like the one that surrounds your brain because this one doesn't have a leak. God! Now I sound like my mom. Sorry," Kevin said.

"Why do you do that, why do you apologize? It was quite funny; you're a comedian in the making. This place, it feels alive."

Yeah, I hear you, Kevin thought. Everything is alive and watching every move we make. We should get out before we forget how.

"Did you say something?" asked Tim.

"No. Did I?" Kevin looked at Tim. Did he just hear my thoughts? His mind started reeling. When I was lying on the ground afraid to open my eyes I smelt the fire, and I could hear it getting close. That's when I thought of sci-fi flicks, about dimensions in time. That's when I saw an old wooden door latched and locked; hardwood reeking with sandalwood. My fingers transformed into keys and I opened it — a door to a parallel universe, a door to a place beyond the flames that is

coming, as sure as eggs are eggs. Then I remembered Tim and my eyes slowly opened. What's going on?

"Whoa!" Tim's jaw dropped. "You didn't move your lips. What the hell? Fair dinkum, K, this is crazy shit. This is awesome. I heard everything," Tim said tapping his head. "In here. This is friggin awesome, dude!"

Tim to K: come in, K? Tim thought.

"Get out of my head! What the hell?" Kevin looked at Tim sideways while rubbing his head as if it hurt.

Kevin thought for a moment. *This, this is kind of cool. But let's keep moving.* In unison they raised their hands in the air, smiled, and high-fived, just like they did when they had been younger.

Finally, they found their way back and stopped at the floating protective membrane. They looked at each other then at the charcoal bushland beyond. The sun was a burnt orange, falling off the face of the earth, and making way for the grand entrance of a full moon. They moved forward together. Tim imagined a crazed pent-up cattle dog making tracks within his mind.

"Relax, man, you're scaring the shit out of me," Kevin said. The dog in his mind sat still. *That's better*, Kevin thought.

"Okay, let's do this," Tim said out loud.

The feeling of each other's fear drifted as they submerged themselves into the membrane. Kevin's eyes closed — his hands were outstretched and he relaxed into the silence of his mind. They floated not wanting to leave, not thinking, just being.

Colors engulfed Tim's mind before he left the seren-ity, stepping onto a burnt log. "Wow, psychedelic, amazing." He watched Kevin still floating, unmoving within the wall.

Kevin was lost and unaware Tim was beyond the wall. An image appeared before him, a deer surrounded by colored light. The sound of chanting and drums echoed in a distant corner of his mind, getting louder. The image evaporated. Kevin jolted, his arm jerked. He was being pulled away and he fought to stay. He didn't want to leave; he felt it was vital to connect. The deer was waiting for him. He felt himself exiting the embryonic state, first his hand, arm, foot, a shoulder, then half his head and chest. Tim pulled him all the way out. Kevin's shoulders slumped, his arms and limbs a dead weight, and the warmth of the dying day caught him off guard. He dropped to his knees and waited while he adjusted to the heat; it scorched the back of his throat and nose with each breath.

"You were in there for at least half an hour, just floating. You fall asleep or what? You looked like you were having a ..."

Kevin wasn't listening. Scattered black mounds paved the way to the river — swollen carcasses, they smelt like they were ready to explode, and a frenzy of flies feasted on the kangaroos. They looked as if they had been lying in the sweltering heat for days. The fire was out. Not a spot fire around or even ash or embers.

"Do you think your dad was here?"

"I don't know." Kevin rested his hands on the back of his head, confused. "How did they get it out so quick? It should be at least still smoldering."

8

PRIMAL SCREAM: SOPHIA. SCOTLAND

The forest looked misty and grey. Sophia was tired of running, tired of being alive in such a cruel world. The ground sloped to the left. It was cooler under the trees. The distant splashing sound of water running over small rocks told her a brook was close by. Sophia couldn't decide which direction it came from. Ahead, in the distance, was an abandoned cabin or an old clan dwelling. It faced east, overlooking the sloping mountainside.

Father McDonald slipped off his pack. "Stay here."

"No, I'm coming with you."

"No. Get behind the trees while I make sure no one is inside. It's still hunting season and someone could be in there."

"We haven't seen anyone for two days," she argued.

"It's best to be safe." He looked sternly into her eyes.

She cast her eyes to the ground, knowing he was right. Two days ago, after hiding from the chaos at the fete, they had munched on the lollies and chocolates that

Mother Catherine had secretly packed for Gemma's slumber party. Recklessly high on sugar and over-confident, they came out of hiding looking for real food, and instead of going around the next town they walked into it.

They pretended to each other that they were on a camping trip, avoiding talking about the massacre at the fete. They craved a hearty Scottish breakfast and needed some camping gear. Traveling along back roads they had seen fewer people. Approaching the outskirts of the town they had passed a small community church alive with the songs of Solomon. The sound faded behind them as they continued on. The streets became quiet again. They passed an empty schoolyard, where a swing moved slightly in the breeze. Half a dozen or so deathly-pale faces paced the sidewalks on the other side of the road as they entered the main street of the town. A few stores were open, making it easy for her and Father McDonald to move about unnoticed. Sophia felt instantly ill with shame. Her legs went to jelly, her vision blurred. She imagined she had given the devil's puppets, the negative angels, an opportunity to see her. Sophia had to stop. She leant against the stone building to catch her breath and waited for the feeling, the ugliness, the absence of light and joy to pass. Sophia guarded her thoughts, holding onto her medallion, thinking of her sisters and better days. Father McDonald pointed out she was resting in front of a camping supplies store.

He pushed open the door to Go Outdoors. A young saleswoman was managing the deserted store. Sophia started babbling, telling the woman Father McDonald was her grandfather and they were heading for the hills until the virus consumed itself. She heard herself, felt out of balance and looked around for a chair.

"You okay?" The young woman came around the counter to help Sophia sit down.

"I'm feeling a little faint. I need to reconnect."

"What an odd thing to say," the store attendant said.

Sophia ignored the young woman and closed her eyes and thought of a tree, visualizing herself nestled into the trunk and its roots going deep into the ground, the branches stretching up and reaching for the heavens. She drew in a long deep breath, and then breathed out, repeating it a few times before opening her eyes. The store attendant handed her a glass of water and a trail mix bar.

"Feeling better? You don't have the virus, do you?" the woman asked, stepping back.

"No, no, I'm fine, really. This is good, thank you."

"No offense, but let's get you two geared up and — out of here. I don't know why I even opened up this morning. We have been closed for three days. Mr McLean, the owner, has disappeared. It was my job to open up on the weekends only. But I had to do something. My parents went to hospital during the army collections, and I haven't seen them since. I was going to go to church. I love singing but I was compelled to come here and open up."

Sophia watched her talking, as if to herself, while picking up backpacks and loading them up with packets of dried food and all the bits and pieces they could possibly need. She would have shoved in a kitchen sink if she had one. She even picked up

Sophia's day-pack and stuffed it into one of the larger backpacks.

"Remember, autumn is around the corner," she said. "Don't stay up in the mountains too long. If it comes over colder than usual as it did last year, you'll end up snowed in for winter, and nobody will find you until the thaw."

The bags ready to go, she helped Father McDonald with a set of hiking poles. "You sure you're fit enough, grandpa?" Not waiting for a reply she turned to the shoe section and plucked a pair of Canadian red leather hiking boots off the shelf for Sophia.

Listening to the woman, Sophia started to feel better. She wanted to believe in her own tale: that Father McDonald was her grandfather. Sophia walked up and down the aisle in her new boots and swiveled around to her captive audience of two. "Perfect fit. Totally comfortable. I feel a bounce, and my heel is pushed forward in motion, making me want to move." Sophia thrust her foot out in a ballet pose.

Screams in the street broke into the peace of the store; like a tremor, a crevasse split open and zigzagged down Sophia's spine. Windows across the street shattered and so did the false reality Sophia had indulged in. She was fearful that this was the way it was going to always be. The screams were real enough and here she was thinking of herself. She twisted around towards the sound, craning her neck. The street seemed clear. Cars were parked against the sidewalk, empty — not a soul in sight.

Sophia, Father McDonald and the store attendant moved to the shop's front window to scan the street, straining to see where the screams originated. From the direction of the church, eight, maybe twelve people came running towards them. Sophia froze; her mind went back to the fete — back to the car park — back to the shots that had exploded in her ears. The sight of Mother Catherine's swollen face, choking. *He's followed us,* she thought.

On the street with each fired shot, someone dropped in mid-stride. Car lights flashed across the street. A man switched off his car alarm, reached out for the door handle and his head exploded, blood and tissue spoiling the roof of the white Golf. Two other people made it to their vehicles and the cars roared into life, screeching out of town.

No thoughts to the fallen. Every man for himself. A mother carrying her baby in a sling across her chest ran along the sidewalk towards the camping store. Sophia could now see the gunman. It wasn't the same guy from the fete. He was older, roundish, dressed like he lived in the mountains and wore the same gear all year round. He carried two rifles — one was slung over his shoulder and he was firing the other.

Sophia felt the terror from the woman heading towards them. Sophia's knees went weak; her bladder filled with heat that spread over her body. A primal scream clawed at her throat. *Move damn it, Sophia, move!* she screamed to herself.

Sophia bolted out of the store to help the woman and her baby. Father McDonald yelled at her to stop, but it was too late. A shot was fired and the camping store window cracked, but held. Her focus was on the woman; Sophia grabbed her by the arm and guided her into the safety of the store, pushing her towards a rack of thermal jackets. Another shot was fired; the air suddenly was filled with tiny crystals. *It was like being in a snow globe.* Time moved elegantly slowly. The glass pierced Sophia's face and hands. She shut her eyes tight and screamed in pain. Father McDonald pulled her towards him. They took shelter together with the woman and baby amongst the thermal jackets.

A car exploded and the building's foundations shook. Sophia slowly opened her eyes; she could see. The panic eased. She stole a glimpse between the jackets and saw a ball of flames, black smoke billowing into the sky. The gunman was jumped on by two men from behind. They crash-tackled him to the ground, pinning him beneath them. They jumped to their feet and started kicking him. Other people joined in. The hunter had become the prey. Sophia had to turn away. Picking at the pieces of glass in her hands, she winced. Her face hurt from the tiny shards of glass embedded in her cheeks. She looked at the lady, dusted the glass off her shoulders away from the baby, and did her best to smile. "Your baby will be okay."

Father McDonald quickly picked what glass he could off Sophia's cheek and said, "Are you okay? Don't do things like that, you'll give me a heart attack. Come on, we have to go."

He looked at the store attendant. "Please help this woman and her child. I am sorry we cannot stay. We have to go. God will be with you. Bless you." Father McDonald wanted to help but he knew the only way to truly help was to follow God's lead and take care of Sophia. "Where is the delivery entrance?"

The young shop attendant pointed to the back of the store.

Father McDonald struggled to pick up the heavy backpack. Sophia saw his thin legs straining. She pretended not to notice as he mustered as much strength as he could and heaved the bag up and fumbled to fasten the waist support straps. He pulled them tight, which took some pressure off his shoulders. Sophia took charge of her backpack and sat it on the bench. She sat down to insert her arms into it and stood up feeling weak. She was more worried for Father McDonald than herself. She wasted no more time and wove between the shelved merchandise to the delivery entrance and headed into the woods.

As soon as there was enough distance between them and any town, Father McDonald sat Sophia down on her backpack while he fished through his bag for a first- aid kit. He had trouble getting the clasp to open on the little red plastic box. Sophia helped him and handed him the tweezers. He started to gently pull out embedded shards of glass. Her face cleaned, he gently laid tiny strips of tape over the wounds. Without a word, they headed deeper into the forest heading south towards England.

IT HAD TAKEN them two days to get here and now the guiding sun was dipping over the horizon. With the load off his back, he said, "A few fishing lessons for you, a rabbit trap here and there and we should manage quite nicely for a few weeks. Now — wait here. Don't go anywhere but if something happens to me — run."

Sophia waited behind the trees watching him struggling painfully up the small hill to the cabin. *He thinks I don't see him take his pills.* Father McDonald stopped to rub his aching hip, pulled out his worn Bible, and continued. There was no one in the cabin, she knew that, but she knew he needed to be sure. Sophia wished she could take away his pain. He placed his hand on his knee to push on up the hill. He wasn't prepared for anyone who meant them harm; there wouldn't really be anything he could do. He struggled forward, believing in God, believing in his guidance and protection. He just needed time to rest; they both needed time to rest and this small log cabin looked like the perfect place. He stopped again and pulled his pills from his pocket, catching his breath, taking a tablet to calm his heart. At the top he stopped and looked out beyond. His shoulders went back and he stood straight. His gaze swept the area admiringly. *Bless you, God, thank you for looking after him,* she thought.

Sophia waited behind the tree as Father McDonald instructed. The air was dense. An acute feeling of being watched crept over Sophia, a new and scary sensation.

Sophia remembered when she first started to control her energy and her ability to leave her body and astral travel. She would fight to overcome her desire to leave this realm and go to the next. At that time, Sister Clare spied obsessively on her and Father McDonald. This is what it felt like now, like someone was spying on her. She missed Mother Catherine, who had protected and loved her, and wished she was back at the church, lying on the pews, gazing at the stained-glass windows.

She scanned the area, but could see nothing, so she scanned again — this time with her sixth sense and she could now feel a calm rhythmic heartbeat. Whoever it was wasn't scared of her. The energy felt gentle. A wave of fragrance reminded her of the scent of fresh lilies and the way some flower petals can float on a breeze. It had to be an animal and it had to be behind her. With a ballerina's grace she pivoted slowly, careful not to make any noise. Over her right shoulder, standing in the distance and hiding in the shadows, was a white deer. It didn't move — it just kept watching. Sophia closed her eyes with the image of the deer projected onto the back of her eyelids and stepped out of her body. Her body dropped quickly to the ground. She felt nothing. Sophia looked at Father McDonald and saw he was still laboring towards the cabin.

At ease in her spiritual body, Sophia moved silently amongst the trees. The deer's ears perked up and its nose thrust forward, smelling the air, sensing Sophia's youthful spirit. Sophia moved closer and stretched out her ethereal hand to the deer. It bowed. Sophia's hand slowly moved down its neck, over its muscular shoulder, and along its silky back. Sophia's bewilderment melted as their souls united. Sophia was in awe of the dainty lady-like energy it possessed, and the warmth of its body. She could feel the tenderness of the deer's thoughts. It was ... Sophia struggled for the right word ... *dazzled*; yes, it was dazzled at how easily Sophia had shed her skin. But Sophia was even more bewildered than the deer. She heard its thoughts, like a parent, in her heart: *You must be careful. Your youth fools you. You are truly old, and must take greater care of your physical body, or someone or something might take it.*

Sophia, finding her inner voice, said, There is nobody around. No evil dark cloud and no lost souls. Sophia felt embarrassed. But you are right. Thank you for your concern.

Come, I'll walk back with you to your body.

Together they crossed the path of fallen leaves. Sophia hugged the deer, then infused herself back into her sleeping body. She felt the heaviness of the physical world, the phenomenal limiting pressure of the five senses. She wiggled her toes and fingers before opening her eyes. The deer was licking her face with its rough tongue. Sophia wiped the sticky saliva off her face and rose to hug the deer with all her physical strength. She could no longer hear its thoughts, but still felt the essence of its celestial being.

Father McDonald was calling out: "Sophia, Sophia!" Suddenly a bright flash radiated from her locket, which had captured the sun's rays and, laser-like, shone in his direction, blinding him. He shielded his eyes as the beautiful deer stepped out from behind the sphere of light. Standing on the porch, he waved again, giving her the all-clear.

Sophia threaded her arms through the harness of her heavy backpack, and stood up. A squirrel darted down the near-by tree trunk, startling her as it leapt into her path. She sensed the squirrel's laughter as she stumbled. The white deer didn't flinch. An eagle screamed overhead and they all glanced up. The eagle circled the air above the cabin and rose up and over the mountains. Father McDonald began to speak into the sky.

Sophia couldn't hear the words, but watched as his lips moved over the familiar passage. "He that dwells in the secret place of the most High shall abide under the shadow of the Almighty. He shall cover you with his feathers, and under his wings shall you trust: his truth shall be your shield and buckler." Sophia remembered this was from Psalm 91.

Sophia walked up the hill to stand beside Father McDonald on the porch and together they watched the eagle until it was out of sight. *I think we could call this place home for a while,* she thought. The white deer circled the cabin then walked away to the sounds of the flowing river.

"Come on. Let's get this place cleaned up," Father McDonald said, resting his arm on her shoulders.

Sophia followed him into the cabin. *It was well kept and rather modern on the inside. Obviously someone's furnished holiday cabin.* In a glance off to the left she could see a wood-burning stove in the kitchen, a small bench and hanging pots, a plastic white sink with a pump action lever and, against the wall, a kitchen table for two. It was a tiny cabin. On the right side was the living room where there was a sofa covered in dusty sheets facing an open fireplace. Off to one side of the lounge room, a narrow wooden staircase went straight up to a lofty bedroom. Under the stairs, facing the lounge room was a bathroom.

"I'm going to check under the cabin for a generator," Father McDonald said. "With this much stuff there has to be one." Father McDonald walked around the outside of the building and quickly returned, puffing, exhausted.

"That was quick. Any luck?"

"No." He walked slowly into the kitchen surveying the tiny space and finding a trapdoor under the table. Together they dragged the table away from the wall and he pulled on the metal latch. It resisted and he stopped and held his back. "I'm not as strong as I used to be." Nerve pain fired from the base of his spine to the top of his neck. "I'll be right in a minute or two."

Frightened, Sophia guided him to a chair and said. "Maybe you should rest here." Over the past week his body had visibly aged. Sophia pulled on the latch, flipping the door up, and searched the kitchen drawers, finding a working torch.

Father McDonald rose and took it from her. Slowly he climbed down the narrow stairs. He ducked, just missing banging his head against the wooden frame. "You go find yourself a bed. I'll be right," he said, as he descended.

Sophia knew there would be no arguing, and ran up the steps to the loft. There was a double bed and two singles. She picked the single that lay under the skylight and she lay down to watch the sky above for a while. Reluctantly she rose, opening the window for some fresh air.

THEY CLEANED the dust off the furniture and aired the cabin, unpacked only what they needed in case they had to move quickly. They settled down the best they could. Sophia threw the sleeping bags on the beds and made up Father McDonald's to be as comfortable as possible.

The night came round quickly while they were busy cleaning and collecting wood. The generator now provided a comforting hum and, more importantly, lights. A can of hot chicken soup tasted and smelt smokey from the wood stove. Sophia cleaned their bowls and Father McDonald went and sat on the porch to read from his Bible. The outside world faded away as his warm, harmonious voice floated in through the open door. Sophia listened while boiling pots of water and pouring them into the bath. The vapors of steam rising from the surface of the water looked inviting, but she resisted the urge to climb in. "Father, come see."

Wearily he stood in the doorway and said, "You're a gem. Thank you for the bath, Sophia. It's just what I need. God bless you."

Sophia waited until Father McDonald climbed the stairs for bed. "Feeling better?" she asked.

"Totally rejuvenated."

Sophia quickly had a cold shallow bath, just enough water to wash the dirt out of her hair. Shivering, she climbed out and dried herself with the new half-size microfiber towel the storekeeper had packed. Sophia put on her second-hand dark-blue and yellow tracksuit. It looked like new and she remembered why she had packed it in the first place and started to cry. She sat on the edge of the bath and waited till her body stopped heaving. She wiped her eyes with the back of her hand and towel-dried her long hair as best she could. She felt better for the tears and better for her bath, even if it was freezing cold.

Sophia lay down on her bed and cocooned herself in the soft familiar textures of her sleeping bag. The forest was alive with sound and the cabin was dark. Stars shone through the skylight window between a few fallen leaves. There were streams of dazzling stars and four stars glowed brighter than the rest.

"You awake? Can you see the stars?" she asked Father McDonald.

"Yes."

"Do you know the names of the four stars shaped in a cross?"

"I can't see those through my window."

"Come see."

He groaned quietly as he unfolded his body and shuffled over to her bed. She made room for him to lie beside her.

"See," she said pointing into the sky.

"Marvelous, it's beautiful — Blessed are you, Lord. That's the Grand Cross, Sophia, it's very rare. There's Mars, Pluto, Jupiter and Uranus. They should be at ninety degrees from each other, I think. Throughout history, significant events like revolutions, the start and end of wars have occurred at such times. Sadly, these planets in this formation have become a symbol of pain and suffering. A great strain has fallen upon humanity, there's no denying it. It doesn't matter what happened in the past, what matters is the future. It may be a sign of great darkness, but it can also mean there is potential for even greater light. We are going to need a lot of mercy and compassion in the coming month for ourselves, and the world so it seems. The stars hold many secrets, Sophia. In the book of Matthew, astrologers from the east followed a star to Bethlehem, for the birth of Jesus."

Without taking his eyes off the stars he recited, "The Lord is my shepherd; I shall not lack. He makes me to lie down in green pastures: he leads me beside the still waters. He restores my soul: he leads me in paths of righteousness for his name's sake. Yea, though I walk through the valley of the shadow of death, I will fear no evil: for you are with me; your rod and your staff, they comfort me. You prepare a table before me in the presence of my enemies: you anoint my head with oil; my cup runs over. Surely goodness and mercy shall follow me all the days of my life: and I will dwell in the house of the Lord forever. Amen."

"Amen." Sophia didn't want to dwell on the significance of the Grand Cross. She heard and understood what Father McDonald had said, but right now she just wanted to gaze at the stars and imagine what it would be like to sail amongst them. "How do you know so much about the stars?" she said.

"I was in the navy, and many nights I prayed to God under a blanket of stars. The early seamen navigated only by the stars, believing in myths and legends. You can always find your way home if you know how to read them. Now get some sleep. God willing, tomorrow I will show you how to fish."

"I would love kippers!"

"I don't think it will be kippers."

He must have thought she was fast asleep and, careful

not to wake her, he unceremoniously slid off the bed with a thud. She clenched her teeth imagining the pain rippling through his hip. He picked up his torch and headed down the stairs. He took some painkillers out of the side pocket of his backpack, and went outside. Under the light of the moon, Sophia watched as he switched on his torch and hung it from the wooden beam above. As the shadows watched, Father McDonald nestled the Bible in his two hands and read out loud into the night: "You shall not be afraid of the terror by night; nor for the arrow that flies by day: Nor of the pestilence that walks in darkness; nor of the destruction that wastes at noonday. A thousand shall fall at your side, and ten thousand at your right hand; but it shall not come near you."

He leant against a post and rested his eyes. The book fell between his knees as he drifted off to sleep. Night after night he read on the porch until the morning chased away the shadows and the world gave birth to a new day.

9

DOORWAYS TO A PARALLEL DIMENSION: SHAUN AND KEVIN. AUSTRALIA

A smoky blood-red sky covered the city. The air was thick with vermin. They were in his house, they flew around his bed and blocked out the light from his soul. Soaked with sweat, Shaun tossed and turned; flames licked at his bare skin, the heat blinding his vision as he dreamed of burning alive. Under his eyelids his eyes darted back and forth.

"*RACHEL!*" he screamed as loud as he could, but only a whisper escaped his lips. Out of breath, he woke, panicking, gripping the bed, his heart pounding against his ribs and tears trailing down his cheeks. He wiped his face with the filthy sheet. The images had already dissolved, the dream forgotten, but the fear remained. Shaun reached for the comfort of his mobile phone, accidentally knocking it to the floor. He shuffled into the bathroom, coughing a little. His father lay passed out on the lounge room floor, an empty bottle of whiskey still clasped in his hand. Shaun quietly stepped over his body and looked down in disgust. The desire to stomp his heel into his father's face and pay him back for the beatings and pain his mother had endured was compelling, but the thought of his mother stopped him. His foot landed on the carpet, nearly clipping the tip of his dad's nose. He walked sluggishly into the kitchen.

Shaun jerked opened the refrigerator. The light came on and his hand flew up to protect his eyes from the sudden glare. The milk was sour, the bread moldy, and the Vegemite empty. He slammed the door shut. Miserable, he went upstairs and climbed through the attic to the roof. In his boxers, he lay stretched in the early morning sun and tried to remember what it felt like to lie beside her and smell her perfumed hair.

"WHAT? What the hell do you want with me, boy?"

Shaun woke disoriented and nearly rolled into the gutter and over the edge of the roof hearing his dad's voice. Gingerly, he moved to look over the edge. There was a fireman at the door. Shaun leant a little further and slipped on a loose tile, catching himself before he went over the edge. The dude looked up, and Shaun ducked out of sight. *Shit! How could they know?* he thought. He strained to hear their words.

"I saw the bike on the lawn yesterday," Daniel said. "Do you know whose bike it is?"

"What bike? I don't know."

The fireman turned and pointed to the sky-blue bike resting on the lawn. "What about your son. Can we ask him?"

"What?"

"Is that your son's bike?"

"No. Now piss off!"

The door slammed an inch from the fireman's nose. He walked down the porch stairs turned and looked back up at the roof. Shaun lay flat trying to melt into the roof and his cheek slapped against the warm roof tile. He heard something moving beside him and twisted his neck around to see a creepy, dark flickering cloud, caught in the stream of sunlight stretched across the sky. It was like looking through a microscope at squiggles of organisms. He blinked and they were gone. His skin crawled; the atmosphere was gritty and tasted metallic. He had tasted something like it before. Suddenly he found himself falling. Instinctively, to break his fall, he pushed his hands out in front, and something sharp jabbed and sliced into his palm. He winced in pain and pushed himself up. He glared at the blood in his palm, a gash clean and straight as a surgeon's knife, right along an old forgotten scar. There was nothing on the roof that could have made a clean cut. Tiny black flickers like worms danced around his head. He waved his hands through them and they disappeared.

"What the hell?" he said. He looked back at the road. The fireman had picked up the bike, thrown it in the back of the Dodge and driven off.

"Shaun! Shaun!" his father yelled through the house.

Shaun stayed on the roof and waited for him to shut up. He felt the cool morning summer breeze dry the salty fluid from his body. Smoke rolled down from the mountains like a fog rolling in from the ocean. Shaun tuned out his father's ranting. In the distance a black streaming cloud twisted hypnotically. It reminded him of something. It felt important but still nothing came. It had been like this on and off for years. It drove him insane.

He slithered off the side of the roof and back into the house through his bedroom window. He put on his t-shirt and jeans and slipped into his runners. He opened up his top drawer and stared at the leather pouch. He felt it with his fingertips and drew in a jagged breath. It was worn and shiny from his handling, and still had the smell of a tannery. He picked it up and felt the shape of the stones, shoved it deep into his front pocket and climbed back out the window.

TIM WADED INTO THE WATER. "Hey, that reminds me, K. You're sleeping at mine tonight. We're not going to have to deal with your mom at all."

"Yeah, you're right".

They dove into the river and swam, using the tide to carry them across. Their bikes and clothes were gone. The bush was deathly quiet. The light was being sucked out of the day. They walked along the blackened trail and stopped where the anthill had been. "Something's not right," Kevin said. He walked on to the end of the track and stopped to look back at the charcoal trees. He didn't need to hear Tim's thoughts to feel his unease. They headed for the vacant lot; the tall grass had been burnt down to the ground. Barefoot, spiked vegetation jabbed their soles as they walked towards the empty street ahead.

❧

Kevin saw Tim's mother was in the kitchen gazing out the window. She saw them walk across the backyard and waved.

She smacked a kiss on Tim's cheek before the back door closed. "Hi, boys. Sorry I missed you both last night," she said, returning to her cooking. "I got home so late, I didn't want to wake you."

Puzzled, Tim's eyebrows hiked up towards his hairline and looked as if his mom had lost the plot. His sister walked into the kitchen and bumped hard into his shoulder. "What was that for?" Tim said, rubbing it.

"Don't you two start," his mother snapped, rinsing broccoli. "There is enough violence on the streets. If you don't have something nice to say to each other, then I'd advise you to say nothing at all."

"I'm going to my room," Kathy said. She paused just before the kitchen door closed, and beckoned to the boys to follow.

Tim's mom wiped her hands on the tea towel and opened the refrigerator. "I've made some rocky road for you guys to take tonight." She retrieved a Tupperware container and flashed it around the room.

"Kevin, your mom was looking for you. She was hoping you'll be home before dark to pitch the tent. You'll have to get a move on if you don't want to disappoint her."

Kevin finished the glass of water and put it on the edge of the sink. He gave Tim a confused look.

"Okay, Mom," Tim said. "But we're —"

Kathy launched back into the kitchen and pulled Tim out of the room before he could say anything else.

When they were out of earshot, Kathy said, "Where the hell have you been? Mom may think you were tucked in your bed last night, but I know you weren't!"

"You're crazy," Tim whispered. "What are you babbling about — you came to my room to give me a tenner this morning, so you could go out with some douchebag."

"That was yesterday, and where's your bike? I saw you from my window walking along the street. And where are your clothes?"

"What! Yesterday! What's today? So, that's why my mom was here." Kevin said. "We've lost a day. We've been gone over twenty-four hours. That's why there was no smoldering bush. I'd better get home. Grab your tent."

Kathy followed them to Tim's room, watching them scramble around for the tent, flashlight, sleeping bag and pillow. "What do you mean you've lost a day? Tim! What's going on?"

Kevin picked up his unopened backpack. His mom had packed extra things. He could tell by the way it was tied and bulging out the sides. She still treated him like a kid, which he found annoying. *But sometimes it is nice,* he admitted to himself. He felt a pang of sadness, thinking that she was trapped by her own fears. *That's the true plague*, he thought and walked out of Tim's room.

Kathy flicked the hall light on and off. "Guys? Guys?"

They stopped at the top of the stairs and turned to her.

"What now?" Tim asked.

Kath looked at them as if they were a pair of idiots. "You owe me that ten back, or I'll let the cat out the bag," she said.

"You can be a real bitch," Tim said.

"Oh, and maybe you guys are used to hanging out in your underwear, but perhaps the few neighbors left don't need to know."

"Oh, shit," Tim said, dropping his things in the hall.

They rushed back to his bedroom. Tim opened his drawers and fished out two pairs of cargo pants, one blue and one khaki and two white Bonds t-shirts. He handed Kevin a shirt and the khaki pants. Tim pulled on his sneakers and tossed a spare pair to Kevin.

Kevin's nose wrinkled in disgust and his eyes began to water. "They reek! I'm not wearing them."

Tim didn't want to part with his Nikes. "Oh, man! Okay. You so much as scuff the toes, you owe me a new pair." They grabbed their stuff and bolted down the stairs.

"Bye, Mom."

Watching the news, his mother called absently, "Aren't you forgetting something?" She heard them go into the kitchen and collect the rocky road out of the icebox. She remained in the plush leather recliner and pushed out her cheek for a kiss, not taking her attention away from the television. She was focused on the dark-haired reporter with the deep baritone voice. He was an American reporting a missing person.

"Over a year ago, Professor Ellen Freeman, a leader in genetics research, went missing from her lab and remains to this day unaccounted for. Twenty-four hours ago it was reported to police that her daughter was kidnapped. Her last known whereabouts was Myrtle Beach, South Carolina. The police are questioning the young man who reported her missing and they are trying to locate her father. They are treating the circumstances as suspicious. With the majority of the police force dealing with the violent-infected, it's unlikely there will be an extensive search conducted."

"Hey, Kevin, didn't your mom go to Carolina?" Tim's mom said.

"Yep, and she never talks about it."

Tim sat on the arm of the chair. "Wow, the girl's gone now. I reckon the father did them in. What do you think?"

"Tim! That's terrible. You have no idea what that poor family are going through. Don't be so quick to judge."

"Sorry, Mom. Let's go, K."

MOST OF THE morning Shaun wandered around the semi-deserted city, staying away from places where people might recognize him, and he rode the trains all afternoon. *I'm just the local bully, son of the drunkard. Son of a diseased woman who died, leaving me to defend for myself against what my father had become, a drunken thief. But dad hasn't always been a drunk.* His dad had loved her so much, his spirit had died with her.

Shaun enjoyed being on trains because he didn't have

to keep up an image and he mostly pretended to be asleep. Sometimes he could even believe his mother was sitting next to him. They used to travel into the city by train to see a movie before the cancer took over their lives. They would have lunch and buy a toy in the magic shop, or a book from the bookstore. He remembered walking into the grand old theatre, the walls lined with statues, his mother bought ice-cream, chocolate or popcorn, he stared at the statues wishing for them to move. They were the good times before she died. Shouts from the front of the carriage woke Shaun from his daydream. The passengers who had boarded the train at the last stop looked more than just tired. The train had only just pulled out of the station when they started arguing over who was going to get the window seat, and if the window should be open or closed. Then abruptly an old dude from across the aisle had stood up and slammed the window shut, pulverizing the guy's fingers. Shaun wasn't going to inhale the same air as those sorry-looking infected assholes any longer and jumped off at the next stop. Walking home, he picked up some groceries along the way.

He waited at the threshold of his home and listened; the house was empty. Satisfied, he hummed as he went into the kitchen and put away the bread, milk and Vegemite. He always felt better after riding the trains, but he decided he would give it a miss for a while, because more people were getting sick. *And what was with the old dude's black pupils.* He had seen shows on the TV where morons tattooed their eyeballs, but this was different somehow.

FROM HIS BEDROOM Shaun heard the front door close. His father stumbled through the house into the kitchen knocking a glass off the bench. *Drunk again,* Shaun thought, as he changed the sheets on his bed. His stomach grumbled; he was starving, but he would wait for his dad to fall asleep. Shaun opened up his sock drawer and put the leather pouch way at the back, ignoring his tummy. *Fuck him, why should I hide,* he thought, making his way to the kitchen. He quickly cooked six pieces of toast and spread butter and Vegemite on three, and peanut butter and jam on the rest. He wrapped them up in paper towels, grabbed a bottle of coke and closed the fridge door with his foot before heading up onto the roof.

He heard the toilet flushing and leant over the edge of the roof. The back door opened and his dad, half-dressed, puffing on a cigarette, dropped a bag of rubbish into the bin. Shaun worked up a mouthful of saliva and let it hang from his mouth into a strung-out spit, and sucked it back up. He did it again, letting it grow a little longer, a little thinner and a little lower before sucking it back up. He did it again til it was too thin, too long and gravity took hold: it was heading for his dad's back. His dad stepped forward and flicked his butt into the garden and the saliva splatted onto the pavement behind him. His dad looked up. Shaun had no time to move back, so he kept still, not wanting his dad to think he was frightened. *I can take a good beating,* he thought.

"You filthy bugger — you lazy good-for-nothing. Why don't you piss off?"

"Why don't you take a look at yourself, old man? I never understood what Mom saw in you. You're a cluster-fuck. Weren't you supposed to be some big-shot professor? You're a pathetic fraud. You let her die."

"You ungrateful prick. I should have left you to die with your little girlfriend." He picked up the shiny lid of the garbage can and threw it up into Shaun's face. Shaun ducked and just missed being scalped, but the lid skimmed his cheek and sliced it open. Shaun dropped to his knees, holding his cheek, holding in the urge to scream with pain, because he wasn't going to give his old man the satisfaction. "Fuck, you're a dick!"

"Not so tough now are you, kiddo?" his father said, slamming the back door closed. The street was empty of all other sounds.

Shaun looked down at his hand, covered with blood. "Ah, shit." He pressed it against his face, walked to the edge of the roof and climbed over the eaves and down the drainpipe.

KEVIN AND TIM walked as fast as they could down the quiet street. "What are you going to tell your dad about your bike, K?"

"I'll just say I couldn't carry all this stuff. That's not going to be a problem, but something is ... I can feel my dad ... something's not right, he's worried."

"Hey, look." Tim pointed towards the row of houses.

"What?"

"On the roof over there. Some guy is on the roof."

The fading light of the sun shone on a miniature flying saucer that shot up into the sky from the back of the house, smacking hard into the dude's head. He had his back to Kevin and Tim so all they could see was a silhouette drop to his knees, going down like a bag of potatoes. They ran across the road, watching him standing at the edge of the roof, trying to steady himself before sliding dangerously down the side of the house.

"Hey man, are you okay?" Kevin called.

The guy turned around at the sound of Kevin's voice.

Kevin continued to walk across the street and Tim grabbed his arm. "Wait, K, that's the guy that kicked the shit out of me. Stuff him, let's get out of here."

"Chill, man, we can't — he's seen us, act cool."

"You okay?" Kevin walking across the lawn. He could see the blood dripping between the boy's fingers and face. Shaun pretended he didn't recognize the other two boys. However, he couldn't stop eyeballing Tim's leg. Then Shaun staggered, trying to focus on his mobile phone; he was having trouble swiping it unlocked. The sound of a car coming around the corner and stopping at the curb seemed familiar to Kevin. He turned to see it was his dad. Kevin turned back to Shaun. "You'd better go inside and get some help. Are your parents home?" Shaun grabbed Kevin's wrist with a vice-like grip and said, "No one's home, so just piss off." Then his legs buckled as he blacked out and collapsed.

"Wow." Tim looked down at Shaun's face. "His eye

and cheek are already swelling. Look at that, he looks like he just went a round with Mike Tyson."

A car door slammed. "Kevin!"

"Dad." Kevin ran over to him. "Get your first-aid kit."

"What?"

"Your first-aid kit."

Daniel reached into the back of the Dodge and pulled out the green bag with a white cross on it from under the seat. "What happened?"

"He was on the roof and was hit by a piece of flying metal. His cheek's cut and it's bleeding pretty badly. He just dropped."

Daniel knelt beside Shaun and went to work checking his vitals and looking for serious injuries.

Tim tilted his head towards Kevin, half whispering, "Irony or what!"

"Kevin, sit behind Shaun's head," Daniel said. "Hold the dressing against his cheek like this. Tim, call an ambulance." Daniel handed his mobile over.

Kevin watched his dad go to work. As soon as Tim was through to the emergency operator he put the phone on speaker and Daniel took over. *Shaun didn't look so tough lying unconscious,* Kevin thought.

It took a while for the ambulance to arrive and when it did it coasted silently down the street, afraid of the infected. The ambulance staff feared being hijacked for their drugs and equipment. *Shaun was probably lucky they showed up at all.*

There was a low-pitched buzzing high above that was getting closer. Nobody else seemed to notice. Kevin felt like he wanted to run, but he dared not move. He sensed long dirty fingernails plucking at his soul. He wanted to run screaming like a lunatic from the property. The urge was becoming so great he had trouble keeping still — his whole body itched. Out of the corner of his eye he believed he saw a curtain move inside Shaun's house. Kevin kept looking straight ahead, acting as if he was watching the ambos crossing the lawn. The muscles in his eyes strained to see in his peripheral vision. Someone and something was watching them. A shadow, a dark mass inches from the ground, moving like a school of fish, curved and shifted around the side of the house, slithering out of sight. Kevin felt dryness in his throat. A heaviness he hadn't detected until now came from the house. He concentrated on holding Shaun's head, waiting for the ambo guy to take over, and soon as he did Kevin stepped back. His skin still prickled and his stomach churned. He could feel the haunting pulse of the house. He pulled his thoughts away. He was scared and wanted to run. In the back of his mind he saw a lemon tree, it grew and grew until he felt he was part of the tree and suddenly he could smell lemongrass and sage. He took in a deep breath and tried to calm down and focus on helping Shaun.

"Tim!" Kevin whispered. He tilted his head towards the house. "Someone's watching." Daniel was giving the paramedics a summary of Shaun's injury and Kevin listened to his dad speaking, sounding muffled as if he was deep underwater. The ambos crouched beside Shaun and carried out the same procedures as his dad had previously done. Kevin watched, but heard nothing.

They slid Shaun onto an orange plastic board and hoisted him up onto the gurney.

"Kevin," Daniel said. "Kevin!" He put his hand on his son's shoulder and squeezed.

"Yeah ... what?"

"You okay? Why are you shouting?"

"Sorry. I'm good."

Daniel bent his face down and looked closely into Kevin's. "You up to riding in the back with your friend? If he wakes up, he will at least see a friendly face?"

"What ... yeah sure; if I have to."

Tim chuckled.

"What are you giggling about? I don't think there is anything here to be laughed at," Daniel said. "Chuck your stuff in the back with the bike and get in the car."

Surprised, Tim said, "You got Kevin's bike?"

Daniel opened the car door. "I saw it last night. I drove by this morning and it was still here so I picked it up. Is that why you three were fighting? Did Kevin come over to pick up the bike? Did you guys hit that kid?"

"You think Kevin smashed him — no way. Kevin wouldn't hurt a fly, in any case."

"I didn't think so, but had to ask."

Just before Kevin climbed into the back of the ambulance Tim ran around the front of the Dodge and purposely bumped into him and whispered in his ear: "Friendly face, ha, ha. Better you than me, K. If I see the ambulance swerving all over the road I'll know the feral cat woke and saw your friendly face, ha ha ha."

~

THE EMERGENCY WAITING room was packed. People were coming in and hardly anyone was going out. A mother came in carrying her young boy; his arm looked like an S-curve. He was white as a ghost and looked like he was about to upchuck. Many people were coughing, rubbing their heads, or trying to blow their noses. A pregnant teenager was crying, heaving into a plastic bag, while her caring mother held back her hair. The little boy with the broken arm was taken through the door marked Triage. A man stood up aggressively and pushed his way over to the reception's plastic anti-jump barrier and banged his fist. "Hey, what's the deal? We've been waiting for two hours and that kid gets in."

"Please sit down, sir."

Agitated, the man rubbing his head yelled at the small woman behind the barrier. "He had a broken arm!"

Both hands went up to his head as if it would burst. "I can't think straight any more. I just want to see a doctor."

"Sir, calm down and go look after your wife."

The security door to the treating area opened. Kevin could see his dad shaking the doctor's hand and together they entered the waiting area talking. He could hear his dad saying, "Okay, thanks for your help. We'll pop in tomorrow and see how he's doing. Let's go, boys," Daniel said, putting a hand on Kevin's shoulder.

The doctor walked to the vending machine and watched his coffee being dispensed.

"I've asked you nicely, sir," the lady behind the barrier said. "Now I'm going to get security."

Kevin left the emergency area through the sliding doors when, abruptly, he stopped, becoming increasingly aware of the angry man walking back to his wife. "Shit," Kevin said running back inside and nearly tripping over Tim. "*Move!*"

"K, where you going?" Tim said.

Kevin's sneakers squeaked loudly in his mind as he ran along the blue spongy linoleum floor and thought, *Why do they call them sneakers?* Security guys lazily entered the waiting room from the same door his dad had used. They were chatting casually, tucking in their shirts and hiking up their utility belts, totally blind to what was about to happen. *Shit,* Kevin thought. Everything seemed to be in slow motion again. The colors around the angry man who had been yelling at the receptionist changed to a black, oily swirl as he strode over towards his wife, who was weak with fever, her beautifully colored hijab soaked. "Stop," Kevin shouted. But it was too late. The man's face was clammy, his hair greasy. Kevin reached for him and smelt stale perspiration as he grabbed the back of the man's shirt. His wife tried to pull away as her husband snatched her arm off her chest, snapping her wrist. The woman shrieked in pain.

The man yelled back at the receptionist, "Now can we get some attention around here?"

The doctor abandoned his coffee and rushed to the woman. The security guards pushed Kevin to the floor before tackling the man to the ground. Most people sat by as if this was normal; people didn't seem to care any more. Kevin felt his dad reach down and help him up.

Daniel dusted his son off. "You okay? How did you know? What were you thinking? Let's get you out of here. Let security do their job."

Kevin doubled over and held his stomach. "I feel sick. I can still feel her pain." He ran outside and threw up on the pavement.

Daniel rubbed Kevin's back until he stopped throwing up. "I'm sorry, Kevin," Daniel said. "I don't know why this happens to you."

Kevin wiped his mouth with the ends of his shirt. "I'm okay."

Trying to lighten the mood, Tim yelled like a circus ringmaster with his arms up in the air. "Ladies and gentlemen, the quantum psycho virus has come to town!"

"I don't doubt that, Tim, but you don't have to yell it out," Daniel said. "I have been dealing with this sort of shit all week. So many guys at work have called in sick and we are running skeleton crews just like the cops. I thought being on the other side of the world had its benefits. It's been a few years since it started and I thought, given the time and distance, it might have died out, and we would have escaped it altogether, or with little casualties. Like the old bird flu."

"Anything's possible, just got to have certainty, Dad." Kevin looked away embarrassed, not knowing where the thought came from, or why he said it. It didn't feel like his. "Whatever," Kevin said, trying to cover up his confusion.

"That's what your nanna used to say. Kevin, don't ever be ashamed of your abilities, be proud. You're a good person. Tomorrow we will come back to see your mate. I don't want you guys coming into the city on your bikes. Or using the train by yourselves." They all got in the truck and he turned on the ignition. "The city is a crazy place at the moment. You don't know who is going to turn."

At the mention of his bike, Kevin felt a knot in his stomach. He was going to have to tell his dad he lost it. "My bike ..." Kevin mouthed to Tim.

"It's in the back," Tim mouthed back and thumbed over his shoulder towards the tail of the truck.

"What?" Kevin lifted his hands and shrugged his shoulders, shaking his head to imply he didn't understand.

"What are you guys going on about?" Daniel said.

"I was just telling Kevin, you have his bike in the back."

"Ah, yes. I saw it lying at the front of Shaun's and picked it up. I didn't know you knew Shaun. Hope I didn't cause you any problems. I know he is a little older than you both, but I think that boy has had a hard life. It's nice you guys have made him your friend. Just don't let him influence you to do — well, I think you know what I mean. Stay out of trouble."

TIM HELPED Kevin grab the tent out of the truck, while Mr D lifted Kevin's bike out and propped it against the garage wall. As they walked through the garage door and into the house, Kevin called out, "Alex! You home, buddy?"

"We're up here. He's in the bath," Mrs D replied.

They dropped their stuff at the front door and climbed the stairs.

"Hi, Mom, sorry I'm late."

"Hi, Tim," Callie said ignoring Kevin. "Did you have fun last night?" Callie continued rinsing soap out of Molly's hair."

"Oh yes, thank you. Did you hear that your US professor's daughter is now missing, too?" Tim said.

Kevin held his breath as her facial muscles tensed.

"We saw it earlier at my place, on TV," Tim said.

"We're just going to pitch the tent. It won't take long and Alex can come down after he has finished his bath," Kevin said.

"Go get some dinner. I wanted you home before it was dark." She turned and looked at him. "Is that blood on your shirt?" she said lifting Molly out of the bath.

Kevin looked at his shirt.

Tim could feel the tension building; Kevin became a mess, instantly looking guilty and ashamed. He felt sorry for him and jumped in to rescue his friend. "That's right, it's blood," Tim said. "A kid got his cheek sliced open. Then Mr D arrived and took him to the hospital. K —"

"Tim, it's Kevin, not K."

"Sorry." Kevin was holding a cloth to his face. Tim was dying inside. He wanted to rush his sentences, was starting to feel like he was lying and that he was to blame for all the shit in the world. How did she do it? Just then Kevin's dad walked in and saved them.

"The boys were genuine heroes this evening," Daniel said, lifting Alex out of the bath and wrapping him in a towel. "Kevin tried to step in and stop a man from breaking his wife's arm. He obviously foresaw it because he started charging at the man before it even happened. Well done, K."

Tim's eyes darted to Kevin's mom, to see if she would react to Kevin's dad calling him K — *go, Mr D* — but she was distracted.

"What do you mean, *foresaw*?"

You could cut the air with a knife, Tim thought, and now Mr D is going to take the tongue-lashing she had been saving for Kevin. "Let's go," Tim whispered to Kevin.

"It's too late for Alex, Kevin," his mom said. "It's nearly his bedtime."

Alex started to whine. "*Oh pleeeeeeease, Mommy, pleeeeeease.*"

Molly copied Alex. "*Peasss, peasss.*"

"Off you go, Alex," Daniel said, overruling Callie. "Get your pajamas on, and your robe and slippers."

"But it's not cold, Daddy," Alex said.

"No robe and slippers, no tent. I'll come and get you in half an hour," Daniel said.

The boys turned on their heels and made tracks outside, Alex in tow. They pitched the tent close to the house. They had so much to talk about, so the wait for Kevin's dad to fetch Alex for bed seemed like hours. They sat in the middle of the tent devouring chunks of rocky road and patiently telling Alex fart jokes.

"'NIGHT, boys, don't stay up all night gasbagging. You hear anything strange you get inside. You shouldn't be out here. We'll go early to the hospital, before my shift starts."

"Night, Dad."

"'Night, Mr D."

Kevin strained his ears, listening to his father's footsteps crunching across the dry back lawn, waiting to hear him step onto the patio and into the house.

"What —"

"Shh." Kevin put up his hand to stop Tim saying another word. As soon as the outside light was turned off he said, "Now we can talk."

"What a crazy day, man. I'm never going to get to sleep. My leg was crushed! We magically survived a firestorm, ignited by that dick lying in the hospital. Now we have to go and see him tomorrow."

"Did you see him looking at your leg? He knew who we were."

"What happened yesterday, K? Where did we go? We have to go back. We have to go back and find that place. Everything was electrifying. The fluorescent colors — awesome, dude. And my leg, my leg, it just, it just healed and the sunburn vanished. What gives? And don't forget my shoulder dislocated. Man, all that shit hurt. What was that, a vortex?" Tim was nearly out of his sleeping bag, nearly on top of Kevin, and with each question, he spoke a little faster, a little more excitedly. "Everything was connected, even us. You heard my thoughts."

"I know, right. How bizarre was that, totally unbelievable!" Kevin drifted into his own thoughts and spoke contemplatively, Tim hanging on his every word. "I don't know what happened," Kevin said. "I believe it was very real, as real as it was when I saw the boy drown. The wall — it just appeared. The smell of smoke was the first thing I noticed. I then saw you, and the rest is just a blur. We needed to escape the fire — I needed to get you out of there. I couldn't see how. The fire was surrounding us. I kept looking. Then I saw what I first thought was an illusion; I was concussed from the king- hit. I got up and touched the wall. The shimmering mirage sparkled like a lake in the midday summer sun. I pushed my hand into it, and when I pulled it out, the sunburn was gone. I had no doubt, I was certain this was our way out. A door to another dimension had opened up to us and I didn't want to think about it logically, because there was no other choice."

The soft glow of the streetlight and a cluster of silhouettes swayed hypnotically across the dome of the tent. He watched Tim touch his leg and stretch it upward. He flexed his knee, making sure it still worked.

"Do you know anyone named Jade?" Kevin asked.

"Nah. Why?"

"I don't know," Kevin said, closing his eyes. "When we were leaving and we were in that, like, embryonic jelly state, before you pulled me out, I thought of the name, and I saw some other things, but I can't remember clearly."

Kevin and Tim talked and talked, throwing out one idea after another about where they could have been. Exhausted, Tim finally fell asleep mid-sentence, and Kevin crashed three ideas after. The night cooled as he slept on top of his sleeping bag and dreamed of the day's events.

10

INFECTED: CASEY. ENGLAND

Casey stretched, feeling refreshed and comfortable in the motel's feathered bed. *Now for a famous English breakfast,* he thought. He dressed and rushed downstairs to the buffet, soon sitting down to a mountain of eggs, sausages, mushrooms, potato cakes and a side plate of muffins. Terry and Amy drank their strong tea and watched him wolf it down. The motel was quiet and there were only two other couples at breakfast. Full of food, the trio headed into the lobby and waited for the solicitor.

Gary, the UK solicitor, acted like a tour guide, pointing out the sights as they drove through England into the north. Casey was glued to the window, mesmerized by the lush rolling hills and fields of yellow poppies as they headed to Amy's inherited estate. Snow might be falling in a few weeks and he shivered at the thought of the temperature pushing past zero and beyond. He loved the warmth of the sun.

The car pulled off the road onto a dirt driveway that

was hidden by green hedges. Silver birch trees lined up on either side of the road and the fallen leaves were scattered by the movement of the car. He started to feel a cold sweat rush over him as they moved closer to the end of the driveway. The car stopped and Casey flung open the car door and vomited.

Amy came up beside him patting his back. Casey wiped his mouth and said, "One sausage too many."

"You're pale as a ghost!" Amy said.

He rested his hands on his hips, straightened up and drew in a deep breath. *I can do this*, he thought, *but I wish Sophia would hurry*. Running his fingers though his hair he said, "I'm okay. Check this place out, Amy. This isn't a cottage. This is a manor."

Ivy climbed the walls and arched across the entrance. The thatched roof looked old but well maintained. Casey shoved his hands deep inside his pockets, digging his nails into his leg.

"It has eighteen rooms in all," the solicitor said, "with a cellar, and a shed that was once a stable."

Terry held onto Amy's hand and said, "This is wonderful. I had no idea it would be so big, did you?"

"None, I can't believe it's ours," Amy said. "Can you smell the trees, and the grass? It smells so fresh and crisp."

"That's good old English air. My dad used to say it would put hairs on your chest. Shall we go inside?" said Gary, the solicitor.

They moved from room to room admiring the furniture and the decor. Casey walked behind Amy and Terry into the kitchen. "The smell's not as fresh in here, bit musty." *It feels like someone is here, like we're intruding,* Casey thought. The atmosphere was thick and the air stale; a shiver ran down his spine. "It's so cold, is there any heating?"

"There are six open fireplaces in the house: one downstairs in the living room, another in the library, one in the master bedroom and two in the double bedrooms," Gary announced. "Amy, your great-aunt only used a small part of the cottage. The story is that once the arthritis clamped around her fragile bones she settled into the downstairs rooms. Nobody has lived upstairs for at least five years." He kept talking as he walked out of the house. The trio followed. "A cleaner used to come once a week and her son chopped the wood. The woodpile is big enough to keep you warm for two winters. Sometimes you will be snowed in. There is a snowmobile out in the shed. Do you have any questions?" Gary's shoes crunched on the gravel as he turned around to face the road. "Oh, and you can get general supplies at the wee town about twenty miles south, that way," he said, "and the ocean is that way."

"All of this is mine. You sure?"

"Yes, ma'am, everything in the buildings and every bit of the land from the beginning of the drive to the fences in the back paddock. From time to time you'll see some fine Shetland ponies grazing. They're not yours; they belong to the family two paddocks south, but with this virus, they have left them to roam just in case, well, you know ... Oh, one more thing: there's an old Jaguar, a Jeep SUV, and a Bonneville in the shed. The keys are in the library desk drawer. Now, if you have no more questions

I'll take my leave. My family are heeding the Queen's advice and seeking safe harbor in the countryside, as are you. Until, well, I am sure you know as much as I. Good luck and God bless".

"What's a Bonneville?" Casey asked, glad to be outside. He watched as the man smiled and bounced on the spot.

"What's a Bonneville? Young man, you haven't lived till you've been on a Bonneville. It's a classic Triumph motorcycle. I'm sure you'll take a shine to it, if your dad can pull himself away from it, because I'm sure he will fall in love with it. Maybe he'll teach you how to ride it one day."

Terry, Amy and Casey looked at each other, but no one spoke.

"Right then, I'll be off." He opened the car door and climbed in, fastening his seat belt.

"When is the cleaner due?" Terry asked him through the window.

"I gave her a tinkle, no reply. There's no cell phone reception here by the way; you need to use the landline. Her number and address is on the library desk. He waved calling, "Cheerio, God bless," as he hurriedly drove the vehicle around the garden and headed down the drive, leaving the trio, gobsmacked, on the steps of their new home.

OVER THE PAST FEW WEEKS, settling in the house had been fun. It was a little cold but a place Casey felt he could call home. His room was awesome, huge with four double-sized in-built bunk beds, a writing desk and a window seat that looked out over the moors.

He saw Terry reverse the SUV out of the shed ready to head into town for supplies. Casey grabbed a light jacket before he ran downstairs to join him.

Standing out front of the manor, Casey looked over at the birch trees towards the quiet road while Amy was saying goodbye. She pecked them both on the cheek.

"We'll be back soon," Terry said.

Terry scooped up Amy, kissing her passionately. Casey felt a little awkward as he leant against the car and stared up into the gloomy sky. *Will they ever get over each other?* he wondered. It was kind of sick that they were still mad for each other.

"I know, just be careful," Amy said patting Terry on the arm. "Have you got the list? Get two months' worth and — don't ask me why two months." Amy raised her hand to block any protests. "I feel a crescendo; the human race can't go on like this forever. Something's got to give." With a sudden change in tone, like the cat that got the cream, and a smile in her eyes, she said, "Oh, one more thing." She pushed her hand into the pocket of her slacks and pulled out a second list. This one was a smaller piece of paper. "I nearly forgot. Can you also get me these things?" She handed the list to Terry.

Casey sensed she was up to something. He watched the colors change around her, from the electric blue covering her throat, to swirling yellows and oranges, and shifting to peaches and pink. Her aura became a blaze of pastels that flowed out to Terry. Casey walked around the front of the SUV to the passenger side smiling, giving them some space.

Terry looked down at the list and started reading out loud. "Night light, nappies and safari wall decal ..." He looked up at her, confused. "Casey doesn't need a night light, he's practically a man." Nearly inaudible, he said, "Incontinence?"

Casey shook his head, trying not to listen. He couldn't help thinking about this morning's media update; they had had a fleeting satellite connection and the broadcast was really an update of death. Few people found compassion and nursed their loved ones. Many people were abandoned to the crumbling city hospital systems. The infected, the possessed, roamed the streets, terrorizing everyone who didn't have the sense to stay indoors. Images of abandoned, feral children filled the screen. The reporter said parents who feared being murdered in the night would strap their infected children to beds. Once-infected people didn't seem to really recover; they were merely shells of their former selves, empty puppets waiting for the puppeteers of hell to claim them.

Terry had said, "Mass suicides are making Jonestown in the 70s look minuscule. Thousands are dying weekly. They believe God has abandoned them, or that God is calling them home and so are taking their own lives. No country has been left untouched. One infected man in particular claimed to be the soul of Christ and persuaded four thousand *uninfected* men, women and children to poison themselves together while online. And, of course, the media hounds latch onto these stories and broadcast their latest opinion poll: to suicide or not to suicide. The

Children of the Stars cult believed suicide was necessary for their final transition and they needed to shed the human form to go back to their place among the stars; they believed their forefathers, the aliens, brought the plague to stimulate them to transcend this world."

"Suicide is never the answer. Love is," Amy had said.

Casey, Terry and Amy were shocked at the reporter's lack of empathy, the three of them had stood transfixed in front of the screen.

"God help them all," Terry had said.

Casey noticed his thoughts straying again, and snapped back to the present.

"How long have you had the problem?" Terry was asking Amy. She shook her head and put her finger to Terry's lips.

"Shh."

"Of course, it's a personal matter and I shouldn't bring it up in front of Casey. It might embarrass the lad."

"Terry! You're killing me!" Casey said.

Amy looked down at the ground. "I was thinking of making this place more homely." She looked up and expanded her arms and swept her surroundings. "I like the idea of staying here more and more. Everything is so green and alive. You can apply for a teaching job here if the schools reopen ... I shouldn't say if, but *when*. I think it might be a good place to raise a child."

Terry looked at Casey and back at Amy. "I'd hardly call him a child."

"Don't look at me," Casey said, leaning against the front fender. Casey knew what Amy was trying to say and couldn't believe someone as intelligent as Terry could be so thick. Casey chuckled to himself, shaking his head in disbelief.

Terry looked back at Amy, feeling like he was missing something. Then she took his hand and placed it on her tummy and the penny finally dropped. Wide-eyed and with a grin from ear to ear he said, "Are you sure?"

Amy tilted her head to the side, looked him in the eyes and smiled. "Yes! I'm sure. That second list is for the baby store."

Terry picked her up and spun her around and around then safely delivered her back onto solid ground. "How far?"

"Nearly three months," she said, holding on to steady herself. "You'd better head off and get the supplies. Last week the old women were nattering in the general store, saying the army was going from town to town taking food and killing infected."

Terry kissed Amy rapidly on the cheeks. He lost his footing, and slid on the grass, catching himself before falling. They were both giddy, laughing with joy.

"Congratulations, guys." Casey gave Amy a hug and Terry a manly pat on the back.

"Thank you," Amy said hugging Casey back. "You will make a wonderful big brother. You have a lot of pestering to look forward to."

"Funny, Amy, funny. Sometimes you guys are so lame. Come on, Terry," Casey said, dragging him towards the SUV.

Terry gave Amy one last hug and kiss. "I can't believe we're going to finally have a baby." Then he remembered the world had gone to hell and maybe a baby wasn't such a good idea at all.

IT TOOK fifteen minutes to get into town and park in front of the general store. There were three other cars in the lot, and two cats ducking into the dumpster for scraps, but not a person in sight. Casey pushed open the store door. The female store clerk behind the counter didn't register Casey or Terry's presence. Her long, starved face was cast down.

"What's she fixated on?" Casey stepped up to the counter to take a closer look. There was nothing to see but a pair of dirty brown shoes. The woman's aura was dirty brown too. Flickers of dust like micro-metal shavings swarmed around her head. Casey backed away and said softly, "She's infected."

"Let's get what we need and get out of here," Terry said, touching Casey on the elbow, guiding him away from her. Terry ripped the supply list in half and quickly they gathered the items and met back at the front of the store.

Terry was finished first and could see Casey coming up the central aisle. "I'll leave the money on the counter. Go straight out and load up the car."

Casey pushed his trolley out to the parking lot. He hauled the bag of rice and buckets of chocolate and vanilla protein powder into the rear of the SUV. He packed in the dried potato mix, dried eggs, flour and cans of tuna and vegetables. He made room for Terry's load and helped him pack it in. Casey closed the back hatch. "We have everything on the list. Except for the live chicken ... that might be difficult!"

The baby store was on the corner at the other end of the deserted street. Terry parked the car so it was front forward, ready to leave town. Terry admired the buildings, finding in them a special charm. The old, stone heritage cottages were probably part of an earlier estate.

"One of these days," Terry said, looking left and right as if on a busy city street, "I am going to dig into the town's history. This would be a nice place to raise a child. Not too far from the sea, far enough away from the city, and close enough to the hills. Weather's getting extremely overcast and damp; I think a storm's coming."

"I think it might always look like this," Casey said.

Terry pushed the door open. The tiny wind-charm above the door jingled. With one hand on the door he paused, preventing Casey from entering. "Hello, you open, hello?" No one came to greet them. Warily he moved in and Casey followed. Together they walked among the shelves.

"Hey, look at this, Terry." A playful smile stretched across Casey's face, as he held up a strap-on pair of breasts. "Male breast feeding."

"Funny!" Terry said laughing. "Actually, not a bad idea, you could use them too. One size fits all, right."

Casey looked horrified and quickly put them back.

"Very chic for a small town," Terry said. "Where's the owner. Hello! Hello!" Terry was becoming uneasy. "Something's not right. Casey, stay with me." Terry moved towards the back of the store. The sign on the door said, Staff Only.

Casey could see what Terry was about to do and said, "Don't open it."

"I have to."

"Don't. Let's leave the money on the counter like before."

"I have to. Stay behind me." Terry pushed the door open and it banged against something on the floor. He stuck his head through the crack and peered into the darkness. The smell was the first thing to hit them. He held his breath and waited for his eyes to adjust. Exhaling, he pushed harder against the door. "A woman lying on the ground is preventing the door from opening." Terry angled his hip into the gap to squeeze through but hearing a deep growl fill the room, he stopped moving.

"Was that a wild dog?"

Terry withdrew his hip and stuck in his head only.

"What are you doing?"

"I count four sets of yellow eyes in the darkness. I think the woman is dead," Terry said looking back at Casey.

He quickly pulled the door closed and reached for the bookshelves. Terry heaved at the metal shelving, packed with the latest baby books, and began to drag it across the floor.

"Help me, quickly. Get on the other side and push."

Casey directed all his energy to the bookshelf. He felt an electric sensation between his eyes. He started imagining the bookshelf moving, then placed both hands flat against the shelf to give the impression of physically pushing it. Books fell to the floor and the shelf scraped across the painted concrete floor.

"I told you not to open it. Let's take what Amy needs and get out of here." They loaded the back seat with the baby essentials.

"Jump in," Terry said.

"Wait. One more thing." Casey ran to the back of the store and slid to a halt at the pile of books. He rummaged through the heap. The wild dogs were sniffing under the door, gnawing, scratching and banging against it; the shelf wobbled, more books and wooden toys fell, hitting him on the head. The shelf had become lighter, easier to move. Casey scattered the books across the floor until he found the one he was looking for, then sprinted to the exit, grabbing a stuffed bear on his way out. He climbed into the idling SUV and tossed the book and the bear on top of the supplies on the back seat.

Terry looked over his shoulder to see what Casey had thought to be so vital. "Twins! A book about twins? No, you've got to be kidding me? You're not serious ... really, you think?"

"Just in case. Amy will be fine. I'll help. I can clean the house and do the washing while you change the dirty diapers."

"Thanks, pal. Two ... seriously?"

As THEY DROVE HOME Casey stared vacantly out the car window. The sky was absent of life, no birds darting up from the hedges, the road deserted. The SUV turned into the driveway and Casey jumped out to open the gate, securing the latch once Terry was through and then jumped back in the car. They pulled up in front of the house. "Don't leave it here, drive straight into the shed," Casey said looking back over his shoulder at the main road.

Terry held onto the steering wheel and took a long look at Casey. "What is it, what aren't you saying?"

Casey shifted in his seat. "It ... it just doesn't feel right. We need to move it. Trust me."

Terry had come to love Casey like he was his own. "You okay? We will be okay. This virus will blow over, right? We're pretty isolated. The winter should bury it. It will be our first winter here." Terry didn't give Casey time to answer. "Forget I asked." He couldn't imagine the burden Casey carried. "That reminds me we have to find that leak in the basement. Something's got to be causing the rot up into the kitchen."

"I'm good. Just wish I could do more," Casey said.

"You are helping just fine. Don't put so much pressure on yourself." Terry turned off the ignition and jumped out.

Casey still had his seat belt on as Terry opened his door. "What are you doing?"

"It's about time I taught you how to drive. Don't you think?"

"For real!" He didn't need a second invitation. He unbuckled his seat belt and climbed over to the driver's side.

"Okay," Terry said, a little nervous. "The ignition is ..." The car roared into life. "Okay, so you know how to start the car. The brake is on your left and the accelerator is on your right. This lever is the transmission. Put the gear into D, for drive, release the handbrake and the car should start rolling forward. Slowly, push down on the accelerator."

The car bunny-hopped forward until Casey found the right pressure on the pedal. "Now turn the wheel to the right, towards the driveway. Go down to the gate and then I'll get you to stop and back it up to the house."

"This is awesome." Casey was sliding the stick into drive and pressing on the accelerator.

"You're doing good. You can speed up just a little. Feel that kick; that means it's going up a gear. If it was a manual, you would have had to change the gear using a clutch pedal."

The car crawled along the dirt road towards the gate. Casey felt like he was moving faster than he actually was. It felt good, he wanted to keep going, out onto the road, but he knew they had to get back to the house, now wasn't the time.

"Okay, foot off the accelerator and ease your foot onto the brake. Now shift the gear into R and look into this mirror," Terry said, pointing to the one in the middle of the front windscreen. Make sure nothing and nobody is behind you. Arm over the back of the seat, foot off brake, and slowly accelerate."

Again the car jerked and beeped like a truck as it moved backwards towards the tree line. Moments like these, Casey forgot everything troubling. *Terry will be a great dad*, he thought.

"Okay, foot off the accelerator, slowly brake, bring the

car to a stop, pull on the handbrake and put the car in P. Leave it running, jump out and I'll park it in the shed." Terry maneuvered the SUV into the garage, put it in park and pulled on the handbrake. He reached to turn the ignition off, but it was already in the off position.

Casey stood just outside the shed and waited for Terry to pop the back open to get the stuff out. The car was idling in the garage. He was taking too long. Casey ran up to Terry's window. "What's up?"

"The ignition, it's already off. It's in the off position."

Casey's heart started to pound, he quickly touched the car and it stopped idling. "Must have been a delayed reaction," he said.

11

ILLUSIONS: KEVIN. AUSTRALIA

Callie dropped the coffee pod into the machine, opened the blinds and wiped away her tears. The smell of fresh coffee was relaxing. She could see the tent, drooping with moisture. She knew Kevin lay sleeping, safe.

"Morning," Daniel said.

Callie didn't respond. She didn't want Daniel to know she had been crying. She took a sip of coffee.

"Why won't you go back to the research lab?" he asked. "You're better than a mobile pathologist. Why won't you talk to me?" Daniel was getting tired of the bickering and secrets. "What are you running from?"

Callie kept staring out the window and into the yard, watching the stillness of the morning. "Stop. Just stop," she said. "You wouldn't understand. No more, Daniel. Don't bring it up again." Callie put her cup in the sink and, without so much as a glimpse in his direction, walked out into the backyard. The morning smelt of the recent fires and a haze smothered the city. People weren't bothering as much about getting to work. Everyone was either afraid of catching the virus or becoming a victim of someone who had. *If only she could synthesize the formula,* she thought.

Callie pulled the tent peg that kept the front peak taut and let it collapse onto the boys. They kept sleeping. She put it back into place and unzipped the mesh screen. *A two-man tent used to be a lot bigger,* she thought, gently nudging Kevin. "Time to wake up. You've got fifteen minutes before your dad heads off." Kevin stirred, grumbling, pulling the sleeping bag over his head.

Tim stretched, rubbing his eyes. "Good morning, Mrs D, isn't it great to be alive!"

With a look of bewilderment, Callie said, "Morning, Tim, it sure is. See you boys in the kitchen, in ten." Callie let the flap drop and walked back towards the house. *That boy is always happy;* she thought shaking her head and smirking. *Whatever he's on I want some.*

Upstairs in his bedroom, Kevin finished changing his clothes. He slipped into his Nikes while Tim rumbled with Alex on the floor.

"I wish you were my brother, Tim. You always play with me when you come over."

"Yeah, but that's because I have a sister and she never likes to rumble with me."

"Who does she like to rumble with?" Alex asked.

"She likes to rumble with her —"

Kevin kicked Tim in the leg before he could finish. "Good to go?" Kevin asked.

"Guys, downstairs, I'm going to be late for work," Daniel yelled from the foot of the stairs.

Alex held onto Tim's leg and slid across the polished floor as Tim walked down the hall to the stairs.

"Alex — get up!" Callie snapped as she walked across the hall into Molly's bedroom.

Alex jumped to his feet and slipped on his socks, he lost his balance, falling, tilting forward over the edge of the stairs when Kevin reached out and grabbed him from behind. "Alex! Be careful."

"Thanks, K. I'm glad you're my big brother."

"I wouldn't swap you for Tim's sister."

"Guys, come on!" Daniel yelled again.

Kevin yelled downstairs to his dad. "If it's too much trouble, Dad, we don't have to go. We can wait till he comes out of hospital?"

"Come on, guys, I don't think he is going to get many visitors, do you?"

"Um — no, I suppose not." Kevin looked at Tim and shrugged.

They walked down the stairs as if going to a funeral and slowly climbed into the Dodge. Daniel took off as soon as they were buckled up.

"Where is everyone?" Tim said. "Was there an evacuation nobody told us about last night or what."

Brown smog nuzzled against the grey sky making it seem as if it was late in the afternoon. The morning traffic was practically non-existent. The peak hour traffic had reduced by ninety per cent and all the cars seemed to have congregated in the hospital parking lot.

"Why are all these people sleeping in their cars, Dad?"

"I don't know, Kevin. Let me find a place to park around the back at the service entrance and we can find another way in."

Kevin was feeling agitated and itchy. They walked along the service road past a stinking garbage truck. "Do you think it's going to rain?"

Daniel looked up into the sky. "I don't know. It's dark but that doesn't look like a rain cloud. It looks more like a metallic dust storm; it reminds me of iron shavings."

"You mean the ones that we used in science to show the magnetic pulling and repelling forces?" Kevin said.

"Yeah, yeah, I do, I did that when I was at school too. It's good to know some things don't change."

"So that's where Kevin gets his nerdiness from," Tim said. "Like father, like son. I thought it was his mom. Not that you're not smart, Mr. D — it's just that she developed medicine, experimented on blood and stuff. Um, I think I should stop talking now."

"Good idea. She's a geneticist, Tim," Daniel said.

The hospital lawns generally would be littered with med students enjoying a coffee and fresh air before heading back in to finish, or start, a twelve-hour shift. Makeshift tents to treat the infected were lined up across the lawn with military precision. The trio entered the hospital from a side entrance and took the fire stairs up to the ward. "Why does Shaun get a bed when there are so many sick people outside, Mr D? It doesn't seem right."

"They're all infected, quarantined."

"Kevin, you're being quiet."

"I'm okay, Dad."

SHAUN LAY with his back to the door, staring out the hospital double-glazed window. He heard the door open and didn't move, didn't care who it was or why; probably a social worker. He just wanted everyone to get off his case. The last time he was in the hospital was to say goodbye to his mom, but he hadn't been able to do it. She had looked so scary, he was frightened. He didn't want to say goodbye, he wanted her to come home. Now he lay in the same hospital. The nurses had probably called his dad and his dad probably ignored the call; no surprise there. The nurse said he could go home once an adult signed for his discharge otherwise he would have to go with child services. Shaun could see the intruder's reflection in the window. She was a stout woman with a no-nonsense attitude, sitting with a clipboard on her knee and asking him questions. He refused to turn or answer.

"The police have been past your home and your father seems to be out. You're under eighteen and we can't let you go home alone."

"Get out, leave me alone!" Shaun picked up the plastic cup of water and threw it at the woman. She ducked as if she had done this a million times.

"Being rude and yelling will get you nowhere. If you haven't noticed, there are a lot of sick people and no one is going to pay any particular attention to you. So let's stop wasting each other's time and get this over with."

KEVIN WATCHED his dad poke his head around the door on the first floor and then quickly close it. Kevin caught a glimpse and it looked like Central Station. His dad did the same thing on every floor until they reached the fifth. Daniel opened the door, poked his head around then yanked it open wide. The floor was empty. They walked towards a nurses' station.

"What's your friend's last name," Daniel asked, scanning the patient board. "Is it Grady?"

"You know more than me. We hardly know the guy."

"Why would you lend your bike to someone you hardly know? There's his name." Daniel pointed at the nurses' whiteboard and read Shaun's room and bed number.

"Let's just get this visit over with. This place gives me the creeps," Tim said. "Are we in the psych ward? What's with all the yelling? Maybe I should go wait in the car?"

Daniel put one hand on Tim's shoulder and one hand on Kevin's and ushered them down the hall. Kevin realized they were heading in the right direction as soon as he recognized it was Shaun yelling obscenities.

"What the hell!" Daniel said, letting go of the boys' shoulders. He extended his stride, moving faster towards the commotion. He pushed open the door to Shaun's room. "What's going on in here?"

"You know this boy?"

"Well, no, but my boy does." The three boys stared at each other. Tim couldn't help feeling a sense of satisfaction seeing Shaun all banged up.

Shaun saw them as his ticket out of the place. "Hi, guys. Glad you could make it. I was hoping you would swing by."

Kevin glanced at Tim, wondering what Shaun was up to.

"Sorry, I missed your name," Daniel said to the social worker.

"I didn't say. This boy needs an adult to sign for his release and we can't get hold of his parents. Not that I'm surprised. There is a multitude of homeless children right across the city. I don't know why I get up and go to work each day. Nobody else seems to bother."

Daniel was taken back by this woman's lack of compassion. He moved closer and spoke with a soft tone. "His mother died, and I think his father is having a rough time with it," he said.

Kevin didn't know much about Shaun and he was surprised that his dad did.

"A lot of people are dying if you haven't noticed," the woman said in a matter-of-fact way.

Daniel stepped closer to Shaun and examined the stitches in his cheek as he spoke to the social worker. "I saw his dad only yesterday. We had a bit of a catch-up on his porch."

Why would he be talking to Shaun's dad? Kevin thought.

"Well, sir, maybe you can help out on this one. I have an extensive list of displaced kids. It seems that a side effect of the virus is to abandon your children. I thank God I don't have any."

"I don't need nobody's help," Shaun said. "I'll take the train."

"Don't be stupid, boy. You have a broken cheekbone, eight stitches in your face and you can barely see out of that swollen eye. Ludicrous!"

"My dad must have worked last night. He's probably asleep. He sometimes turns off his phone. No need to get twisted about it." Shaun swung his feet over the edge of the bed.

Daniel realized Shaun was trying to make excuses for his dad, who was no doubt home passed out drunk. "That's fine, give me your pen."

"What? What's fine, Dad?" It registered to Kevin what his dad was doing. "No. He can call his own dad. His dad will come sooner or later."

"No, Kevin, it's okay. We'll drop him off," Daniel said and took the social worker's plastic clipboard and signed the documents.

She put the documents and clipboard into a folder, snapped it closed and marched out of the room.

Shaun was out of bed. Groggy, he grabbed his bloody shirt and jeans out of the pink hospital bag. He dropped the gown to the floor and pulled on his smelly clothes. He hadn't even finished buttoning up his jeans as he went for the door.

"Where do you think you're going?" Daniel said.

"Home."

"I said I'll take you and I will. Kevin, help your friend

get his stuff together. I'll call work and let them know I'll be late."

"Okay." Kevin looked around the room to see what could be Shaun's stuff. He watched him shove a wallet and phone in his back pocket; a leather pouch went into his front pocket along with a set of keys. He had no shoes, and there wasn't anything else in the room.

THE THREE BOYS and Daniel walked back to the car, avoiding the chaos at the front entrance.

"How did it happen?" Daniel asked Shaun.

Shaun stared straight ahead out the windshield. "I dunno, I don't remember."

"Kevin and Tim said you were on the roof. Were you?"

"Dunno."

"They said you were struck by a piece of metal."

"They talk too much. What are you, a cop? No, that's right, you're a firey."

"Were you watching me the other day from the roof? How do you know what I do for a crust?"

Shaun didn't answer. He sat in the front of the Dodge next to Daniel, pretending to be asleep. "This is your place, right," Daniel said, turning off the engine.

"Yeah. I'm all right, I don't need an escort." He jumped out of the car and ran to the front door before Daniel could take off his seat belt. He fished his key out of his pocket and let himself in. He leant inside the door, suggesting he was talking to someone — popped back out and gave an all-okay wave. He flipped the bird and quickly shut the door.

Shaun walked around the house, seeing if the coast was clear. He was alone. He went to his bedroom and emptied his pockets onto his bed, then went into the bathroom, closing the door behind him.

He tried to avoid looking in the mirror. He was feeling frustrated and wanted to punch himself in the face for being so weak, and instantly struck out at his reflection, smashing the glass. He looked at his father's razor, transfixed. Shaun turned on the shower, stepped in fully clothed and sat on the floor. He buried his head in his knees and cried. The salt of his tears stung. The bite of the cold water pelting hard against his head and cheeks hurt. He imagined he was in a nuclear decontamination shower. He peeled off his jeans, stamped out of his underwear and yanked his wet shirt over his head. His skin quickly turned red from the battering of the cold water. He lost track of time as he continued to inflict pain upon himself. Eventually, his body went numb. He reached up to the soap holder, and pulled himself up. The cracked vanity mirror distorted his image and he refused to look at himself as he left the bathroom sopping wet, grabbing a clean towel from the hall cupboard. Shaun wrapped the towel around his hips and shook his head like a dog, splashing water onto the walls. Emotionally exhausted, he went into his room and locked the door before collapsing on his bed.

~

Daniel leant out the car window. "I'll see you boys tonight. Stay out of trouble. I'd prefer it if you steered clear of the Grady's for a bit."

"Gladly," Kevin and Tim said in unison and waved Daniel goodbye. As usual, old man Pat was pretending to concentrate on watering his wife's flowers, but Kevin saw that his eyes kept drifting down the road, staring at the same parked black car. He waved to the old guy, who didn't wave back. Kevin's Apollo was still propped up against the garage. "Hop on. We can get your stuff later," Kevin said climbing on his bike.

"Why don't we take your dad's dirt motorbike?"

"Old man Pat's watching and it's not a dirt bike. It's a BMW GS."

"That means squat to me."

"It's an on-road off-road motorbike. You have to have a license to ride it. Dirt bikes you don't. I don't think I could ride it anyway. I would need to use the gutter or a rock to get on and off. Knowing my luck, I'd drop it and not be able to lift it back up."

"You're the luckiest dude I know. You thinketh and so be it. Like your pushbike ... and what about the ice-cream van last summer? Whenever you were craving an ice-cream, it pulled into whatever street we were on, turning on its scary clown music."

"That was summer. The guy was driving down all the streets."

"Well, what about when you wanted to fly your grandpa's plane? Your mom had that research assistant summer-thingy in the US, and you were shipped off to the farm. He let you help with the crop dusting. You got to fly the plane, K."

Tim climbed on the seat and Kevin pedaled standing up, ignoring Tim's constant chatter. The bike wobbled with the extra weight as they entered the street. Kevin steadied the bike, just missing the side mirror of a parked car.

"Go to mine," Tim shouted. "I'll take Kath's old bike. She won't miss it. I'm starved and have to pee anyway."

For the whole time, riding to Tim's place, old man Pat was the only person Kevin saw. He steered the Apollo into Tim's driveway. Tim and Kevin jumped off the bike and raced into the house, using the bathroom and getting a quick feed.

Heading down to the river, the hot sun bored through the dense cluster of clouds. The anthill remained flattened; the stench of rotting kangaroos and wombats harbored a frenzy of flies. Kevin slowly cycled along the dirt road as if it was a cemetery. There was an eerie absence of sound: no crickets, no birds, and even the usual few lizards and slithering brown snakes were gone. Kevin coasted on one pedal, ready to dismount and drop his bike on the sandy embankment. The tide was out and Kevin felt a sense of foreboding. He stopped and took off his shoes, tying the laces together and flinging them over his shoulder. He pushed his bike downstream along the edge of the river.

"Where are you going?" asked Tim following Kevin.

"I'm looking for a good place to cross." The river narrowed and turned a corner. "Remember that time we walked down here and found those guys growing weed; we kept walking, pretending we didn't see them?"

"We were lucky they didn't shoot us. Shit, it's humid. It's not even summer yet."

Kevin stopped where the river offered a sandbank. He bent down to pick up his bike and hoisted it onto his shoulder.

"What are you doing now?" asked Tim.

"I'm taking the Apollo with me. I'm not leaving it behind this time."

Tim looked at his sister's bike, contemplating if it was worth the effort. He came to the conclusion that it was better to carry it than have her pissed at him. He followed Kevin and waded through the shallow water. They helped each other lift the bikes up the embankment and climbed up themselves. They sat amongst the ashes and pulled on their runners. They silently walked back up the river.

"There, the remains of the burnt-out car." Tim dropped Kath's bike on its side.

Kevin kicked down the Apollo's stand, and slowly moved around towards where the veil between the two worlds had been. He scanned for the shimmer of the wall. The passageway, or membrane — whatever it was —wasn't there.

"Where do you think it went, K?"

"I don't know. We didn't imagine it. Your leg is a reminder that it was real. Did you see how Grady looked at you? He thought he was hallucinating."

Tim rubbed his leg, remembering the pain, afraid it might come back.

"I was lying here," Kevin said. "I could hear the animals and feel the trees. I was scared, man. I could hear the roar of the fire, like rolling thunder. I opened my eyes and first saw you. Beyond you, there it was: rich, lush ferns, green and vibrant. Tree trunks hung with moss, some so tall I couldn't see where they ended. Then I felt the heat of the fire, looked back at you and started shitting myself big-time."

Tim stretched out on the ground on his stomach.

"What are you doing?" Kevin said.

"I want to lie down and recreate what happened," Tim said.

"Don't be weird. Get up and let's go, there's nothing here." Kevin started to walk to his bike. *It happened right here! It really was here.*

Tim got up and dusted the ashes off his cargo pants. "Seriously, I think you're the one who created it."

"You've seen too many sci-fi flicks," Kevin scoffed.

Tim pulled Kevin's arm. "Shh. Get down."

They both crouched, listening. They heard voices moving towards them. There wasn't much left of anything to hide behind, so they kept still.

Kevin whispered. "Let's get up. We haven't done anything wrong."

"You're crazy. What if it's Grady and his thugs?"

"It sounds like a couple of men," Kevin whispered. "Come on, they're going to want to know why we're hiding." Kevin stood up, wrestling Tim to his feet. Kevin could see the badge of a fire investigation team on the side of each of their blue shirts. Regardless of the uniform, Kevin knew he had made a mistake. These guys were up to something; they didn't fit with the uniform.

"It's the investigation team," Tim said.

"Tim, something's not right. I've met all the guys at Dad's station. I don't know these guys." Kevin couldn't quite put his finger on it. They didn't have any equipment with them for a start. He saw the two men climb up the embankment and wave at the two boys. They looked European, perhaps Italian, Greek, or maybe Russian, he thought. One was older with short, cropped hair and was taller than the other, who was younger. They were both buffed to the max. Kevin's mind reeled with images from the old mafia movies his grandpa used to watch.

"Hi son, what's your name? What are you doing out here," the older taller man asked.

"Nothing much."

Tim, nodding as if he knew, said, "You must be interested in figuring out how the fire started?" He looked at Kevin who cleared his throat, and Tim got the message to keep his mouth shut.

"Yeah, smart kid." The old guy spoke with a strong accent. "Do you know how the fire started?" he asked, while the other man walked to stand by Kevin and Tim. "Is that your blue bike, son?"

"Who wants to know?" Kevin asked.

"Is that your bike?" the older man said to Tim.

Kevin just walked over to his bike and climbed on casually; Tim mirrored Kevin's movements.

"What's your name, son?" the younger guy asked. His biceps seemed to prevent him from being able to straighten his arms. He held them at an angle.

"Why? Who wants to know?" Kevin asked.

"You're a rude little prick, aren't you? Where do you live?" The old guy stepped forward.

"Down the road," Kevin said, rocking his front wheel back and forwards. Suddenly, coming up through the handlebars Kevin felt a low pulse, a soft hum and could smell sage and lemongrass. He had a metallic taste in his mouth and could hear a scrunching or a slow-tearing Velcro sound.

"Don't get smart, boy. I'll ask you again — what's your name?"

"Look, we didn't start no fires," said Tim.

Kevin frowned at Tim to keep quiet.

"I didn't ask you if you started them, and I don't care."

Kevin's sense of smell heightened and the aroma of dead animals turned his stomach. These men weren't here to investigate the fires, he realized.

"I think you know what we want. I think you both know," he said, looking from one to the other, and then began to undo his buckle. The older guy looked at his partner.

"*Vremaya dlya distsipliny. What you think?*"

"What does that mean?" Tim asked.

"It's Russian; it means it's time for a good whipping. It might jolt your memories."

"You can't do that?" Tim said.

Yes, they can, Kevin thought.

"What's your mother's name?" he said to Kevin.

That's when Kevin started to feel his body changing, becoming lighter. He could feel every atom in his body become alive and all fear evaporated. He felt a strong sense of urgency and was certain of his movements, confident, buzzing, alive. He was again feeling like a solar battery soaking up the sun, feeling its rays energize him, pulsating through his being and he thought, *the universe provides*. Rippling liquid waves appeared behind the older man, suspended in mid-air over the embankment, growing wider and stretching. Kevin's skin tingled. A window, instead of a wall, was opening, a tear in the atmosphere into the parallel world. Kevin felt the coolness of its vapors radiating towards him; his hair puffed out a little. "I know what you want," Kevin said. The older guy had removed his belt and wrapped it around his fist. "See over there, where the burnt-out car is?" He pointed behind Tim, leading them away from the window.

The oldest walked up and stuck his face in Kevin's. "What is it that you think we want?"

"You're looking for how the fire started — right?" Kevin said, playing dumb. "Go check it out, over here." Kevin pedaled over and behind the old car and said, "Come and see." Tim followed Kevin's lead and lapped the car.

The older man reached out for Kevin and missed. He walked over to the burnt-out car, saying, "Get off the bikes!"

Kevin snuck a sideways glance at Tim and nodded. Tim nodded in reply and they pushed down hard on the pedals and took off, riding straight off the edge of the embankment into the shimmering vapors and disappearing. Skidding to a stop and sliding the bike around to face the wall, Kevin saw the guy stumble on the edge of the embankment.

"What the hell!" The youngest and closest of the two men gave chase. He halted at the edge of the river, nearly falling in.

He looked surprised, as if expecting to see Kevin and Tim bogged in the water below.

The older guy came up behind him and called out. "Stupid move, boys. I was told you had your dead mother's brains."

Looking up and down and across the river, the fake fire investigators searched for Kevin and Tim.

"How come they can't see us, K?" Tim whispered.

"Shh! Why do you always ask me everything? I don't know!"

Tim raised his eyebrows and smiled. "Because you usually do know."

"What the hell are those metallic things flying around their heads? Look, it's trailing them like a veil of flies," Kevin said.

"I don't know, a commercial for hay fever. What did they say about your mom?"

"I don't know! Stop asking me all these questions, and how do they know my mom? I think maybe they've been following us. Did you notice the car parked down the road from old man Pat's?"

"The black hummer with the scratches along its side. Yeah, I've seen it at school too. I thought it was that new guy's dad's. The one who started a year ago just after your nanna and pops — well, yeah, I've seen it around."

Kevin watched the men, who were in arm's reach. He wanted to jump them. He was getting pissed off having to hide all the time. He stepped back into the vapor, it felt like silky satin. He calmed down. The feeling reminded him of the edging on Molly's blanket and the fresh new clean-baby smell. His body relaxed and he felt neurons firing in his head, the infinite sparks of life being shared by the embryonic window; nourishing effervescence of light raced through his body, sparks of colors ignited around him, flaring brightly. Tim pulled him back just before he stepped out and into the older guy. He was bigger than any bully at school.

He looks like a gym junkie, K, not a good idea. They probably spot each other when they aren't chasing kids, Tim thought to him.

Kevin was feeling fearless within his parallel world. Hearing Tim's thoughts again, they high-fived and smiled at each other. They kept watching to see if the men sensed their presence.

The shorter, younger man was wearing a bulky smartwatch and he was sweating like a turkey on Christmas day. Kevin was focused on wanting to know how they knew his mom and why they thought she was dead. There was so much about her he didn't know. She was the hardest person to read. She had said to his dad that it was her "fault", because she had kept her family name. Maybe, just maybe they had killed nanna, thinking she was Mom. But why?

"They're not here," the old guy said. "Shit!" He jumped down the embankment into the river and walked across, following Kevin and Tim's tracks, heading downstream. A crow on the other side cawed and a kookaburra sitting on a burnt limb laughed raucously. The younger guy picked up a rock and threw it high. It missed the bird and ricocheted off the side of a tree just missing his own head. He turned around and threaded his belt through the loops of his pants. He looked back to where the boys went airborne.

"Where did they go? That has to be her kid. Best to call it in."

The short man picked up the squeaking radio to mutter a few words in another language and then hung it off his belt.

"Let's get out of here and get some extra hands."

"Yeah, piss off," Tim said. Gym junkie stopped and looked back across the river right at Tim. Tim froze, his eyes widening — his eyebrows raised and he held his breath. The man turned away. Kevin watched Tim's shoulders drop as he let out a sigh of relief.

"They can't see us, Tim. It's just a coincidence."

"There is no such thing as coincidence. My mom says it's just God remaining anonymous."

"No way. My nanna said that too!"

Shaun backed away from the track. He saw the gorillas chasing Kevin and Tim over the embankment and saw them and their bikes disappearing into thin air. The men were heading back in his direction. Shaun ducked behind a charcoal tree waiting for them to pass. He followed the goons to the entrance of the track where a black hummer was parked. They sat talking with the windows down. A hungry, stray German Shepherd, sniffing around for scraps, leapt up and rested its big front paws on the open window. The driver, the tall guy, pulled away from the drooling, panting dog. The other guy freaked out and quickly extended his arm that held a gun with a silencer, and fired. The dog dropped. The driver jumped out of the car, screaming.

"What the hell? It's all over me. You stupid idiot!" He walked around to the back of the car and popped the boot. He wiped himself down with a greasy rag.

"Sorry, boss. It had that look ..." He backed away from the bigger dude. "It had that rabies look, like the animals in the labs, the infected ones. Hey, man, it was seriously fucked-up shit."

"I should shoot you dead! But I can't be bothered cleaning up your sorry ass."

"Why do you reckon we haven't caught this bug? Shit, we've had enough exposure."

"Who said we're not infected?"

Shaun watched them get back in the car. Once the car took off he ran back to the river looking for Kevin and his sidekick, to see if they had returned from wherever they had gone. He walked across the river to where they had disappeared and waited. His head hurt badly and daylight was fading. He eventually passed out from the pain and dehydration and did not stir even as the moon sank and the sun rose.

12

ASTRAL TRAVEL: SOPHIA. SCOTLAND

Morning light streamed into the cabin, settling across Sophia's bed. She woke with the warmth and the brightness of the sun on her face. She opened her eyes and a bird hopped across the skylight and flew into the sky. Sophia rolled over in her sleeping bag. Father McDonald wasn't in bed. She unzipped her sleeping bag, padded across the room to her backpack. She emptied the contents onto her bed, separating the clean from the dirty clothes. Sophia dressed in her second new pair of jeans before she stuffed the dirty items back into the backpack and carried it downstairs for washing. She looked around the cabin. Father McDonald wasn't on the couch, in the kitchen, or the bathroom. She dropped the bag on the floor by the bathroom and stepped towards the open door and into a patch of streaming sunlight. Instantly, she felt the warmth under her feet rise up into her body. She stopped reaching for the door handle, closed her eyes and breathed in the light.

The door squeaked as she stepped outside. Mindful of the noise, she let it go softly and tiptoed across the porch. At the end of the porch on a wooden bench next to a box of kindling Father McDonald sat sleeping. Sophia picked up his fallen Bible, placed it neatly next to him and went back inside. She busied herself in the kitchen making breakfast: a can of corned beef and powdered eggs. The external and internal silence felt great. Nobody's voice in her head but her own; nobody's thoughts or fears coursed through her space. There was no one except her and Father McDonald. *Thank you, God, for the calmness, the lull in my mind,* she thought. Sophia looked beyond the window, into the blue sky, and said, "How you manage hearing the thoughts and prayers of every man, woman and child, I can never begin to imagine. But that's what makes you God. Give my family a big hug with your endless loving mercy. I'm sorry for not wanting to be *me*; it was just hard to find me, to separate from others. Thank you for giving us a place to rest." She stood on tiptoe reaching for the plates in the cupboard high above the sink.

The smell of the food wafted out the kitchen window, waking Father McDonald. "Breakfast," Sophia said, holding two plates. She watched as he pushed his glasses up the bridge of his nose, cleared his throat and slowly unfolded his stiffened joints to heave himself off the bench. He stood stretching, looking out into the distance. Sophia followed his gaze. Between the trees, she could see rolling hills, and suddenly had the impression they had to walk across those hills into England.

"It's a beautiful morning. God bless you."

Sophia sat on the bench placing the two plates beside her. Father McDonald cast his face to the sky. "God send your angels that govern this day to guide the souls of this earth, to seek within their hearts the door to your eternal light. Give them the strength to battle against the virus and fight for their spirit. Many souls in the past few years have been lost to your enemy. I pray you help keep Sophia safe so she may fulfil her purpose. Help us to walk the path of light. Thank you for restoring our soul with the creation of this glorious day. Amen."

"Amen."

Sophia saw the white deer walk into the clearing with the sun shining brightly behind it. "Good morning to you, too," she said and Father McDonald saluted the deer with his Bible in hand.

THE WATER LAPPED around her bare feet. She waited for the tug on her line, for the fish to bite. Fresh water from the mountains flowed down into the river, creating the sound of gentle splashing over rocks. It was blissful. Occasionally an eagle cried above, music to Sophia's ears. From time to time she jerked the fishing line. The hook sported a piece of stale bread. She laughed, as the tiny fish seemed to prefer nibbling on her toes. Two weeks had passed and every day was bright and sunny. Grey clouds circled at night and lightning lit the distant horizon, but every day was beautiful.

Sophia tied her reel to a rock and pressed it into the ground so she didn't need to hold it. She saw the white deer drinking at the water's edge across the lake. She watched until it went back into the woods. Sophia sat next to the rock and reel and daydreamed of living a hot summer's day in a small town in an average house on a street full of kids.

The town generator blew. There were no fans or air conditioning. Screen doors slammed as children rushed onto the streets heading for the lake. She imagined jumping on a push-bike of her very own and riding where the sun would be so hot the tyres nearly stick to the tar and sweat would be dripping from her armpits. A place where there was a lake, with people of all ages camping on top of rocks that overhung the fresh crystal-clear water, shaded by willow trees.

"Pull up ya shorts, Dave," one of the women would yell.

She imagined turning away, shocked at the unclad nannas with the wobbly arms. Sophia smiled to herself, thinking how her friend Gemma might be inclined to stand high up on the edge of the cliff where other kids were throwing themselves into the water, laughing and calling down to Sophia, encouraging her to climb up onto the overhanging rock to join in on the fun. Sophia could see herself huffing and puffing, her nostrils burning with each breath, as she reached her friend. Flies would buzz loudly around her head; she might frantically wave one away as it tried to settle onto the side of her mouth, swatting at it and accidentally slapping herself in the face. Gemma would be in stitches of laughter to Sophia's great delight.

"Jump, I dare you," Gemma would say.

"No, you go first."

Sophia started to feel her pale skin turning lobster red. Not caring how high up it was, yearning to be in the cool crystal-

clear water below, she scanned the water for an empty patch, nearly impossible with most of the town out swimming. Finally, she finds a spot, bends her knees, throws her arms back and dives over the edge. For a moment, she would be free. Splashing into the silky ripples of the river, submerging into silence, Sophia would feel alive, refreshed, and cool, as if pulled just in time from the wicked witch's oven. She continued to daydream, imagining she was floating endlessly under the water, watching big and small fish darting around her legs. Her lungs would eventually push against her ribs, craving oxygen. She wished she could gulp water and extract oxygen just like the fish. Holding her nose, closing her eyes, and seeing her heartbeat getting slower, until giving in and pushing off the bottom of the lake, swimming up through the sun's rays and breaking the surface with her ears popping, her lungs drinking up the air, and nothing would have changed: the sky is still blue, the women would still sit chatting at the river's edge and kids laugh and jump off the rocks. Floating on her back, until she gazed upon a blanket of stars.

In the distance, Father McDonald was calling, pulling her back into reality, back to the cabin by the lake, back to sitting by the rock and fishing line.

"Sophia! Sophia, you alright? Dear God, let her be okay."

Hearing the panic in his voice, she yelled back, "Sorry, sorry. I was just daydreaming." She lifted her rock and gave the line a tug and smiled at the fading image. *One day,* she thought, *I will live on a street with other children in a regular house and have a normal teenage life.*

Sophia looked over her shoulder and saw Father McDonald walking down the embankment.

"What are you smiling about? I am so happy to see you smiling. It lights up your face so beautifully," he said, carefully lowering himself to sit beside her.

"Oh, nothing really. Daydream, that's all," she said and tugged on the line again. "The fish aren't biting today. Not the bread, although they nibble on my toes a lot. It tickles."

"We have some rabbit stew left over," Father McDonald said. "I know it's not your favorite but it's better than going hungry, right?" Her appetite had improved since she had been up in the mountains. She had color in her cheeks.

Sophia smiled at Father McDonald. "Rabbit stew will be good." She felt calm. She had been working on controlling her communication with Casey over the past week. The more inner peace she felt the more she was able to stay in her own body while connecting to the universe, as if she was holding the front door open but not stepping over the threshold. *The white deer would be pleased,* she thought.

Sophia liked the routine they had settled into. Together they would have breakfast; she would tidy while Father McDonald prayed. Afterwards, they would check the traps and fish. In the afternoon, they would both sit quietly on the porch. Father McDonald would pray while Sophia meditated and connected with the oneness of the universe, then Casey. Monday was laundry day. Friday night to Saturday night the world felt lighter. Sophia didn't understand why, it just did. It felt like God's eye was keeping a close watch and pushing the shadows of the dark creatures back. In a couple of weeks, if they could avoid getting the virus or killed by someone who had it, Sophia and Casey would finally meet. She was certain of it. He made her smile; he made her feel good about herself. Her heart skipped a beat when she felt him reach out for her.

God knows why she was so taken by his wild, bushy curls; the teeth of a comb would drop off in fear of being pulled through his mane. She had never known anyone like him before. He controlled his thoughts. Unlike the kids at school, his thoughts had an angelic afterglow of light.

She really hadn't paid much attention at school. Didn't really try too hard; she just wanted the annoying kids to stop shouting and the teachers to stop thinking bad ugly thoughts about them. They gave her a heavy heart and her head was bombarded with their complaining voices. Sophia had believed that she too was bad, because like attracts like, until she realized that she was just like a radio, a receiver, and needed to learn to change the channel or turn down the volume. The past few weeks, her reflections on the past showed her how she had been self-absorbed, always thinking about what she had wanted, and what she didn't have. She never tried to understand the pain of others; she just didn't want to feel pain. She didn't know how to help anyone. She hadn't been able to say anything because people already thought she was weird, living with the nuns. Luckily she had her two friends and they didn't believe she was strange. She had only taken up ballet to please Mother Catherine and now, Gemma, Lisa and Mother Catherine were all gone. How easy it would be to lie down and die; so much harder to truly live. She decided it was right to want to live and she would continue to learn to control the influx of other people's thoughts and help whoever God sent to her, instead of running. First, she must help change whatever has been done to create such evil entities on Earth and do it before there is nobody left and she never hears another's thought again. But she didn't know how to help.

Yesterday, meditating, she had seen pictures in her mind of people as colored silhouettes, their physical bodies surrounded by red, then expanding away from the body and changing to orange, yellow, green, blue, indigo and violet, then lastly, white, just like a rainbow. Golden light was at the center of their being and each golden spark was thousands of tiny atoms. Within the atoms was deeper light, sparks of positive and negative energy: at the heart was the neutron that balanced the two forces, the residence of the soul, and this was where the battle took place inside each infected soul. The positive energy was sparks of white light, and the negative energy was sparks of metallic grey laced with black. The black was multiplying, consuming the white light. In the vision in her mind, each silhouette had been surrounded by darkness, but still the core sparkled, reflecting all the differently colored particles of light. Every atom vibrated, busy with the light. A backdrop of darkness surrounded the body, but it couldn't penetrate the protective rainbow shell. Slowly, a dark spot would grow and an atom was swallowed by the negative force, metastasizing like a cancer spreading throughout the cells, spreading throughout the body, destroying the light. The colors melted away, the shell became jagged until the body was unrecognizable, no distinction of form, just one with the darkness that had surrounded him.

Sophia had wanted to break away from the meditation, to wake up and stare into the blue sky, but then more bodies and more souls appeared, flickering like candles being snuffed out one by one. Sophia had pulled back from the visions, felt the ground beneath her and opened her eyes, leaving the images to disappear into the back of her mind. She remembered the feeling of the tiny fish nibbling at her toes while she recalled the images that haunted her inner world.

Sophia knew time was running out and people were being used like puppets, being fed negative thoughts and feelings, until they would kill one another — and if they didn't, they would end up falling on their own sword. Her dreams showed her the negative energy hiding inside flesh disguised as a virus, but she pushed away the images and thought of a daisy, a big bright beaming daisy, a chain of giant daisies, and her sisters joyfully dancing in a garden where flowers surrounded them and trees bore succulent fruit. A protective cloak of light tightened around Sophia and her medallion was illuminated under her shirt. She shifted a little, being released from the images, and she hugged her knees. Father McDonald wrapped his arm around her shoulders in comfort. Sophia was grateful for the gift of sight and accepted her destiny.

The deer stood on the other side of the river. Father McDonald saw the deer watching and bow her head to

Sophia. "Come, let's get some of that rabbit stew," she said.

They walked, helping each other, back up to the cabin, accompanied by the smell of pine and fresh mulch. Each step scrunched the dry leaves and amplified the silence of the woods. Father McDonald longed to give her ease from her visions, but he could not; it was for her to shoulder alone. It weighed heavily upon him that a child had to carry such painful burdens, but she must fulfil her purpose if she was to be free. They passed the pine tree where the rabbit furs hung. "Tomorrow I think we can make you that pair of moccasins," Father McDonald said as they stepped up together onto the porch.

AN EAGLE CIRCLED high above the cabin while the afternoon birds chirped, jumping along the veranda collecting breadcrumbs. The clanging of the dishes was homely. Sophia stepped out of the cabin drying her hands on a tea towel. Father McDonald pulled out his Bible and randomly opened it.

"Read out loud, Father, please." Sophia hung the tea towel on the rail to dry and stood gazing into the valley.

Father McDonald smiled at her and cleared his throat before he began. "He that dwells in the secret place of the most High shall abide under the shadow of the Almighty. I will say of the LORD, He is my refuge and my fortress: my God; in him will I trust. Surely he shall deliver you from the snare of the fowler, and from the deadly pestilence. He shall cover you with his feathers, and under his wings shalt you trust: his truth shall be your shield and buckler. You shall not be afraid for the terror by night; nor for the arrow that flies by day: Nor for the pestilence that walks in darkness; nor for the destruction that wastes at noonday. A thousand shall fall at your side, and ten thousand at your right hand; but it shall not come near you. Only with your eyes shall you behold and see the reward of the wicked. Because you have made the Lord, who is my refuge, even the most High, your habitation; There shall no evil befall you, neither shall any plague come near your dwelling. For he shall give his angels charge over you, to keep you in all thy ways. They shall bear you up in their hands, lest you dash your foot against a stone. You shall tread upon the lion and adder: the young lion and the serpent shall you trample under feet. Because he has set his love upon me, therefore will I deliver him: I will set him on high, because he has known my name. He shall call upon me, and I will answer him: I will be with him in trouble; I will deliver him, and honor him. With long life will I satisfy him, and show him my salvation. Amen." Father McDonald stopped reading and looked into Sophia's blue eyes and smiled.

"Amen," she said. "Casey's on the other side of those hills."

"I think they could be the Cheviot Hills," said Father McDonald, "which are on the border between Scotland and England. If that's the case, the ocean is to our southeast. When we leave here, we might head in that direction. What do you think?"

"I'm not sure, Father," Sophia said. She sat on the

deck and folded her legs lotus-style, preparing for meditation. "It's hard not to want to stay here."

She closed her eyes, listening to Father McDonald's voice reading words of strength and protection, and called out to Casey. All afternoon she felt him sleeping, popping in and out of her aura; like a cat he brushed past her but recoiled before he actually latched onto her energy. He was gentle as a petal falling on her face. Ripples of love and compassion fanned out from his aura into hers before he jerked back into his own space and time. Again she called out to him. The sound of Father McDonald's voice was fading as she travelled towards Casey, sensing his energy. Excited, she saw him sitting in a darkened lounge room, lightly furnished. The windows had been boarded up, otherwise the sun would have beautifully filled the room.

The overhead lights were on and Casey was sitting at a computer studying the contents on the screen. White noise burst out of the speakers as she came closer. He turned and examined the room. She hadn't been in this room before. It looked cozy with an open fireplace and a sofa you might lose yourself in, she thought.

He kept turning from left to right; she sensed the hairs rising on the back of his neck. "Soph— Sophia, is that you? I can't see you."

Sophia was manifesting as a shimmer in front of the boarded-up window. Millions of scintillating particles of light started to band together and a ghost of a person materialized. It was Sophia. He smiled. "You look radiant, but faint. Your projections are getting weaker," he said, concerned. "Are you okay?"

She could hear his voice in her mind echoing in space. "I'm better than ever," she said. "I'm trying to project without leaving my body, so it's not left vulnerable for a hostile takeover, so to speak, ha ha ha."

"You look more like a hologram," he said.

"You might want to shut down the computer, before the hard drive fries. Where're Amy and Terry?"

"They're boarding the windows in the rooms upstairs."

"How are you guys holding up?"

"Good, considering. Thankfully, we don't have the virus which is the major plus. Are you still up north?"

"Yes. I think we're just a few days away. But I don't believe that it will be easy."

"We can travel to the next town," Casey said. "That's it, though. There are roadblocks on the main road heading north. South, we managed to get a few miles inland before the next roadblock. We've been able go east to the coast and we traveled as far as the Holy Island. Somewhere near a place called Berwick-upon-Tweed the military had a blockade and it was lucky we were in the Jeep; we heard gunfire and quickly headed into the scrub and turned back."

"We have to go to Israel," Sophia said. Her energy pulsed with light.

"What, where?"

"Israel. Jerusalem, I think."

"We can't get into Scotland. You can't get into England. How on earth do you think we can get to the Middle East. And it's not on my bucket list." Casey knew there was a greater purpose in what was going on between them. He wanted to imagine that they were just a guy and a girl having a long-distance relationship.

"Why Israel?" he asked.

"I don't know yet. I'm not sure if it is Israel. I hear an angry man say *dovesti zhenshchinu* and see the Middle East. I keep dreaming of a bracelet and a green gate with a star on it. Show me something," Sophia said.

"Like what?"

"Turning the lights off and on, you choose."

"Okay, well, flickering the lights, we can't do. Terry has boarded up the windows and he thinks there is a problem with the generator every time I practice."

The computer screen started to flicker with white noise. The radio started hissing and a lonely voice came to life broadcasting the latest counting of the dead. They both stared at the radio, and Casey quickly turned it off as if feeling sorry for having a little fun when there were so many people dying.

"Don't stop," Sophia said. "What else? Pick something up." She could see his eyebrows knot together as he focused on the cushion on the lounge. It moved a little, his body trembled; the cushion started wobbling and fell off the lounge.

"Now pick it up," Sophia encouraged. "Go on, Casey, lift it up, You can do so much more than that. But the key is, you need to believe you can; you can control it, rather than it controlling you. You need to clear your mind of any doubts. It's when you think you can't that you won't. Believe you can and you will."

Casey looked up, rubbed his eyes, then brushed his wet palms on his knees, took in a deep breath, and slowly breathed out, channeling energy towards the pillow. Sophia watched the phenomena of energy swirling through the air like liquid towards the cushion, pushing it down. "Lift it, you're squashing it. Flip it like a pancake. Close your eyes and imagine the pillow rising," she said.

Casey sliced into the air with his hand, as if scooping, and the pillow suddenly went straight up and hit the ceiling. It rebounded into the side table knocking the lamp off. The twirling liquid zapped into nothingness.

He rubbed his forehead and pushed back his long curls, revealing his handsome face. "I know ... follow me," he said, and opened the door to the kitchen.

She watched him stare hard towards the barn. An engine roared into life and a Jeep started backing out on its own. Casey was vibrating, buckling under the power of the energy, his hands outstretched as if holding a giant ball and pulling it towards himself. It was too much; he had to stop. He dropped his arms cutting the connection. The Jeep ceased and the kitchen door slammed closed.

"You okay?" Sophia asked, floating closer to him.

From upstairs they could hear movement, tools clanged and banged hard on the upper floor. "Casey, are you okay down there?" Amy called over the railing.

"All good," he called back.

"You're flickering," Casey said to Sophia. "Don't go."

"Are you really okay?" she asked.

"Yes, just tired," he said, moving back into the lounge room. He bent down, picked up the lamp and placed it back on the wooden table. He fluffed the cushion and laid it on the lounge. "What about you?" he said avoiding eye contact.

"I have to go. I am still connected to my physical body. I'm using the body's energy and it is tiring. I've been eating so much, but this uses up tremendous amounts of energy. I wanted to tell you about the gunman in the last town we got supplies from, and the deer in the forest. Next time."

"What gunman? Maybe I can give you a boost?" Casey said scratching his head.

"No, not today. You're exhausted and you need to get better control of the energy. Even though you're tired you're liable to blow me into infinity and I'll never find my way back," she said and smiled.

He blurted out, "How are we going to get to Israel?"

It was too late to answer him. She could feel the link stretching. Saw in his eyes the light around her flickering. She slowly disappeared. She started to travel; it felt like she was hanging onto the end of a stretched elastic band that recoiled sharply back into her body. She landed hard. Her aura contracted, the vibration was painful. Her legs had cramped with pins and needles. Her neck had stiffened as if it was locked in place. Father McDonald was still reading and she concentrated on the sound of his voice as she settled back into her body, returning all on her own. She was pleased how far she had come in such a short time. At the realization she started to cry. Tears trailed down her cheeks: it was still really emotionally exhausting.

FATHER MCDONALD SAT on the bench behind Sophia, watching her body sway slightly. A bird sat on the edge of the plate in Sophia's lap picking off crumbs. More and more birds came and dared to sit close on the rail of the veranda. Some collected in nearby trees, chirping like a group of theater-goers, chatting and getting comfortable before the show started. He thought about Mother Catherine and how she would find his reference amusing. He missed her, her fussing and good intent. He leant back against the wall of the cabin and continued praying for the world's redemption and Sophia's protection as she settled in to her body. He saw her tears and his heart cried with her. He kept reading until her hand went up and wiped her face. She looked at him and her eyes didn't look troubled, they sparkled.

"You okay?" He closed his book and held his dear friend in the palm of his hand. He leant forward and pushed off the bench.

"Starved," she said. Carefully, Sophia lifted one leg at a time, grimacing from the pins and needles. The bird stealing the crumbs off her plate flew away.

"Stay there, I'll get you a cup of tea and a sandwich." He felt just as stiff as Sophia, having not moved the whole two hours she had been gone, so it took him a little longer to get moving again. They sat on the porch eating their sandwiches and drinking the hot tea until the sun disappeared over the horizon.

"WHERE ARE YOU, CASEY?" Amy called from upstairs. "You've been catnapping all day. Come up here and help."

He had sunk into the couch and refused to think of getting up.

"Casey!"

He grabbed the nearest pillow and pushed it against his ear to block out the sound. He was so tired today; he was feeling unmotivated and a little embarrassed. He wondered if Sophia knew he had been showing off. How stupid he'd been to move the Jeep. He seemed like the guys at the gym who tried to impress girls; he never thought himself to be like that. He had preferred track and cycling, being out in the sun. *When the virus has gone and everything is normal I might become a cyclist like Lance Armstrong, without the drugs.* He wondered if he too would be cheating, just by being himself: if people knew he could generate energy and channel it where and when he liked, maybe they'd think he might be using it to make the bicycle go faster. But he wouldn't cheat, because if they caught him they could claim unfair advantage. *But if it came out,* he thought, *that would be the least of his worries.* He would be ashamed and shipped off to some CIA laboratory to be studied. Casey drifted back to sleep to dream he was racing the last mile of the Tour de France when he was suddenly whacked in the face by the pillow. In his mind he fell off his bike just before the finish line and everyone passed him. He was left bleeding on the side of the road watching, nursing his pride.

"Up," Amy said. "Now, unless you're sick — get up! You can't lie around daydreaming all the time. It's difficult for everyone. You can't get out and do things you would like to do, I get it. But you can't lie around doing nothing. Up."

Casey caught the pillow before she planted another playful blow to his head. "And let's not mention how you guys have dragged me across the world away from everything I have ever known."

"Is that what you think?" Amy's eyebrows lifted slightly, looking him straight in the eyes. "Really ... is that what you think, is that how you feel?" She looked concerned, and her shoulders slumped.

Casey saw the pain in her eyes. "No. I'm sorry. That's not ... that was lousy. I shouldn't have said that. It's not how I feel. I just feel, I don't know, I feel trapped. I sometimes feel impatient, like there is something more I should be doing. But I am so scared of whatever it is. I'm afraid of something I am not even aware of. It's like I have eaten something sour and my mouth feels like velvet. I miss my mom and being a kid. I don't feel like a kid any more. I am only fourteen, and I feel forty." Casey swallowed his emotions. "It's like there is a battle somewhere and I need to go and be part of it."

"*Go*? Go where."

"I don't know. Wherever the battle is. But I can't even see the enemy that we are supposed to be fighting. It makes me feel useless, which pisses me off. I feel frustrated."

"Really, we understand precisely. We are living amongst great darkness. We're bound to sense the heaviness and confusion as the world battles the virus. If we start thinking bad thoughts, then that's all we are going to have. We have to create our own reality and ride through this storm. There is no Noah's Ark, or Moses parting the waters. The messiah hasn't arrived, it's up to you," she said pointing to her head. "The greatest battle is within you, Casey. It all starts in here."

"What about getting a boat? We can make it to the ocean."

"Then what? Where would we go?"

"What about Israel?"

"What? Why Israel?"

"Forget it. I don't know what I'm thinking," Casey said, pushing his hair off his brow and letting out a deep sigh.

He knew Amy was aware that he was struggling, wrestling on the inside, but he wasn't going to share any more.

"There're two ways to Israel. You could sail into the North Sea, down to the English Channel, out into the Celtic Sea past France and down around Spain to get to the Mediterranean Sea and up to Israel. But none of us knows anything about sailing and ocean currents. We could also consider driving the Channel Tunnel to France, across Austria, until finally going through Turkey and Syria. Who in their right mind would want to do that? It would take considerable time and planning under normal conditions. We can't drive for more than an hour, Casey, before we are turned back by the army, and we are hindered by the infected. Besides all that, you would have to have a pretty compelling reason to embark on a journey that just might kill you. But, having said that, that's how you can get to Israel, logistically. Oh, and you can also fly, but we would be shot down." Amy turned on her heel and headed for the stairs. "Now, are you coming? Terry could use those growing muscles of yours."

Casey moaned at the prospect of physical labor and followed Amy. He grappled for the banister and hoisted himself up, one stair at a time.

∼

GLAD THE DAY WAS OVER, Casey stretched out in bed, hearing Amy and Terry arguing in their bedroom. The air grilles in the walls filtered sound like an intricate cochlear system. The staff in the past must have had a field day with gossip.

"I'm worried about Casey," Amy was saying. "I'm not sure if he is handling this as well as I thought he was."

"How is he supposed to handle it?" Terry said. "I am having trouble and he is just a boy. I wanted to scream every time there was a report of a tsunami. Every time I saw reporters focusing like leeches on the faces of crying people as they walked amongst the debris searching for survivors, screaming out their loved ones' names, hoping somehow they were alive. Or the earthquakes in California and Japan. The volcano eruptions in Italy and Hawaii. How are any of us supposed to cope? Then there is this goddamn virus. We're being crushed like ants. How is he meant to be coping, Amy? Tell me that?"

"Why are you yelling at me? What? Are we supposed to just give up and die?"

"No, I didn't say that —"

"Well, you might as well have. I'm going downstairs to read my book," she yelled.

Casey pulled the pillow around his ears and focused on the chest of drawers. His eyebrows knitted together as the drawers slid across the floor, screeching like a nail dragged down a chalkboard; it sent a chill down his spine, his body shivered. Casey released the pressure on the pillow, comfortable now he was no longer unintentionally eavesdropping. He had never heard them arguing before and it was toxic. He sensed the cause was the dark cloud hanging above the house, manipulating them, feeding off their anger. He closed his eyes, wandering into sleep thinking about Sophia, hoping she would hurry. *Is she real or is she a ghost? She better be real, or they're all going to die.*

13

INTERDIMENSIONAL TRAVEL: KEVIN.
AUSTRALIA

Comfortable the men weren't coming back, Kevin soaked up his surroundings. The air was cooler in this parallel world, it looked alive, smelt fresh like after a summer storm. He felt safe. He wasn't tired or frightened; his body was relaxed and energized. *Where are we?*

"You're in my head again," Tim said.

Kevin ignored Tim and said, "It's the same place as before, but it's different somehow. It's in a different spot, too. We were on the other side of the burnt-out car."

"I'm telling you, man, you created it."

"Really, wake up! That's ridiculous. Can't you be serious for once? Sometimes I wonder how we became friends."

"Don't put shit on me. We're friends because nobody else would be your friend. Since the first day of school you've been weird; you'd put your parka on before it started raining. You knew when the school bullies were coming and walked the other way. You've known the answers all your life. You'd stand up before the principal even walked in the room. Everyone said that when you saw a kid drown in the river, you were looking for attention. The cops and all the people searching found nothing, no such kid. But for some reason, I believed you. That's why we are friends. That and you like baseball.

"Look at this place, K. It's magical and you created it. No one can see us behind this wall, this waterfall of ... rippling jelly. It's so smooth, and it moves like silk. It's endless. It flows down into the earth, but it doesn't pool, and it's not wet. We are in a cocoon of electrifying energy. This is an image through the lens of a slow shutter. The colors are so transparent and vibrant it's like going into a 3D gaming zone. Man, what I would give to be able to create another world." A bug landed on the back of Tim's hand and he turned it over and over again as he spoke. He touched the tiny transparent wings, giving himself an electric shock.

"I didn't create it."

"Sure you did."

"No. I've just opened a doorway, like some portal." A little blue-winged bug flew above Kevin's head and was quickly joined by another and another. Kevin felt the ground move under his feet and he quickly jumped back.

"A door to where?" Tim asked.

"I don't know," Kevin said, looking at his feet. "The ground smells like earth. The dirt looks rich and moist and the air is filled with aroma. An electric-blue sky can be seen between those giant trees. We can still see the river and the burnt forest, but we can't smell it, or feel it. It's sort of familiar but I get the impression we are far away. It is neither hot nor cold. As magical as this is, it's not reality."

"Yes, it is, because we're here, we're in it," said Tim.

"You can hear my voice inside your head. How is that reality?"

"It belongs in here in this reality. Not out there. How many times have we heard in science that we only use a small percentage of our brains? Maybe it is reality here in this world and in our world too, but we don't know how to access it. We don't know how to jump a level, we can't search for the cheats, this isn't Halo. You have to stop running from yourself, K."

Kevin jumped back. The tree roots had slightly lifted up out of the ground as if shifting position, making themselves more comfortable, nearly knocking Kevin off his feet.

The petite blue-winged creature flew off the back of Tim's hand and landed on the massive tree trunk. Tim's gaze raced up the side of the tree and watched the canopy shake like a wet dog. Birds went flying, as if woken abruptly from an afternoon slumber, squawking loudly, and then peacefully settled back in the foliage as the tree completed its stretch. The roots burrowed back deep into the soil and everything went still for a few seconds.

Kevin looked off into the distance, deep into the forest. He saw a white deer staring at him. Kevin detected the deer before he saw it. Gentleness radiated from the creature, overshadowing everything else. Its surrounding light shone, beckoning him, and he started walking towards it, moving deeper into the foreign world away from the window that led the way home. Tim followed.

"I've seen this deer before," Kevin said. "When we were in the wall, in transition, the first time ... when we were leaving, remember? Moments before you pulled me out, I saw the deer and felt it calling. Remember I told you."

The foliage thickened; iridescent colors bloomed. The blue bugs continued to fly around their heads. Kevin noticed one sat on his shoulder and one was on Tim's crown. The forest would open up — virtually stepping aside for the deer to pass — and then close in behind them. Kevin and Tim were filled with wonder and continued to follow the deer deeper into the forest. The glowing blue creatures flew over and around the deer, settling on its back, taking the form of a human-like fairy, with a set of massive blue transparent wings and elfish ears. You could see its veins the wings were so thin. Kevin was worried that a strong wind would cause them to tear.

They're stronger than they look.

That wasn't Tim, Kevin thought.

No, not me, bro. Do you think it's the deer?

Kevin didn't respond, just waited. But no more was said and their attention was captured by a translucent, pink crystal waterfall, channeled along thirteen streams that pooled together into a sparkling lagoon. A garden surrounded the body of water. Soft voices came from no particular direction, drifting upon the air like a song. The white deer gently stepped off the grass and onto the water. The boys stood at the edge and watched, wondering if they should attempt to follow, wondering if they would sink.

Come, said a voice inside their minds.

Kevin stretched his leg out; his foot hovered over the water. "Here goes!" He didn't plunge straight down like he expected. The water gently lapped at his shoes. It was a weird sensation: his body felt like his blood was carbonated, he felt elated and bubbling with joy. They both followed the deer, experiencing a sensory overload as they walked.

"It's like I've been shaken like a soda bottle and the lid has just popped off," Tim said aloud. *This isn't anything like walking on a waterbed. Where do you think we are going? Maybe we are dead for real this time.*

The blue-winged creature riding upon the deer disappeared into a hundred sparks of flickering light. The deer's long muscular legs disappeared behind the waterfall and into a cave. Kevin was right behind and he was bone-dry. The cave was lit with purple and white crystals. Fifteen feet ahead was the exit, as wide as a bus, and beyond that a row of swaying willow trees. The forest continued sliding back for them to pass. Kevin, looking up, noticed shining stars and a glowing moon in the daytime sky. *How bizarre,* he thought, *this is so cool.*

"Look," Tim said. "It's the wall. We're back where we started."

Kevin soaked up the details of the outer world, making comparisons in his mind. "No, we can't be, look, the trees, they're not burnt. That place isn't home."

Exposed creek-bed rocks and fallen branches covered in moss lay outside the wall and the sky was filled with looming dark clouds. A howl penetrated the rippling liquid membrane. "I think it's Earth," Kevin said. "Maybe we're in a different place."

Kevin looked at Tim. "Can you hear that? Wolves."

The deer turned around and came up behind Kevin, nudging him forward into the wall. He stepped closer scrutinizing the shapes in the dry creek bed; nestled against a fallen tree was a body. The deer nudged him again. The wolf howled louder, closer. "Okay, I get it," he said to the deer. Kevin didn't need to be nudged a third time and stepped into the space between his new world and the next and melted into the bliss. He could stay there forever. The cry of the wolf was louder again, as if right behind him. A sense of urgency sparked every cell in his body and he stepped out. To his credit, Tim was right there by his side. "Stay close," Kevin said.

The drone of annoying insects filled the air. Kevin crouched beside the body and said, "Hello, can you hear me?" The body curled up in a ball, a hooded jacket pulled down over the head, concealing the person's face. The deer came over and nudged at the ball, inciting a moan. The head slowly, as if too heavy, tilted back and the hood fell away. It was a girl. She opened her eyes and saw the boys.

"Hey, you okay?" Kevin asked.

Confused, she tried to scramble to her bare feet, slipping in the mud.

"It's okay," Kevin said. "We're not going to hurt you."

She sat with her back against the log, holding her knees tight against her chest. She looked scared and confused.

"Who are you?" she said. Her hands went straight up to her head as if trying to stop it from exploding. "Oh, my head kills. I think I have a cranial fracture."

"What? You're bleeding," Tim said.

Her long, raven-black hair covered her face as she tried to push herself up. She was weak and dizzy. She sat on her heels and rested for a moment. "Where are we?"

"I don't know," Kevin said. *She's beautiful*, he thought and felt a little uncomfortable, and shifted his feet amongst the fallen leaves. "Who are you?"

"Jade. Who are you and what do you mean, you don't know?" she said, trying to stand up again.

"Hi, Jade. Nice name," Tim said.

"What's he mumbling for?"

"You can talk directly to me, you know. I'm standing right here. Fair dinkum."

"You're a foreigner. You speak funny. Where are you from?" she asked.

Her hair was dirty, caked with blood. Her clothes were filthy and her face, too, but Kevin didn't see any of that.

"K, the deer has gone."

Something's moving in the shadows of the trees, stalking us ... Kevin heard the bay of the wolf and sensed it getting closer, and that's when he saw a black paw, the size of a lion's, step out from beyond the trees behind the girl, growling. Saliva dripped from its sharp teeth, its lips pulled back in a snarl and it snapped its teeth together.

"Don't move."

"We're dead!" Tim mumbled. "What do we do, should we run?"

In a voice that sounded deep and foreign to Tim, Kevin said, "I don't know."

"Why do you always say you don't know? Of course you do, you always know."

"But I don't," Kevin said.

"K, open the door."

"What?" Kevin couldn't take his eyes off the saliva dripping from the wolf's sharp teeth.

"Oh my God, I have been rescued by a pair of retards," Jade said. "If we run, it will get the slowest of us."

"K, open the door!"

The wolf took a step forward.

"Now, K."

Open the door, Kevin said to himself. *I can open the doorway. I don't create the world, but I can access it.* But how, he just didn't know how. Kevin remembered the electric pulse and how the colors resonated with his touch. He imagined the shimmering mirage was before him and it began to manifest into reality. Doubt crept in, and it disappeared. *What shall I do? Nothing? Maybe it's just not going to happen this time, maybe we are all going to die,* and with that thought, Kevin started to feel sick in his stomach. He closed and opened his eyes quickly, as if he had dirt in them, and felt his mind hush. His face started to tingle; he was breathing rapidly, looking deep into the wolf's eyes. Sweat trickled down his spine. His stomach was in knots. A vapor, a ripple, a mirage the size of a basketball grew as transparent liquid waves expanded, flowing up and down hypnotically, between them and the menacing wolf.

"K, have you done it? Stop messing around, we have to go now!" Tim said.

"It isn't big enough for any of us to enter. When it is, we have to step forward, towards the wolf. I'll tell you when."

The wolf began its run, leapt over the fallen tree and lunged.

At the last second, the hole expanded. "Now!" Kevin and Tim jumped, pulling Jade with them through the silky membrane. They all flinched as the wolf howled and snapped its jaws. *It can't see us, but it can still taste our scent in the air.*

JADE FELT Kevin reach in and pull her out of the embryonic state to the other side and instantly she was aware of the change of environment. Her mouth and eyes were wide as she scanned the area from left to right. "This is incredible. This is too much." Jade held her breath and brushed herself off. *Everything is so bright and colorful, it's like a painting.* She felt as if she was being cleaned somehow, on the inside. The beauty of the scintillating purple and emerald-green trees made her weep. The pain of the past year came flooding up and was washed away, healed. It reminded her of the gate with the star. She tried to blink the tears away and saw Great Turtle. Her great-grandmother was holding a seashell full of smoldering sage and was fanning the smoke into the air with a white feather. Then she was gone. Jade's tears of sorrow were replaced with tears of joy; she felt like she was home. Her headache cleared, her pain had gone and the tears stopped. *My body feels so alive!* "Where are we? No, let me guess," she said smiling and biting her lip at the same time.

Tim looked at Kevin. "She wants to guess. This should be interesting."

"I know, don't tell me. This is so abstruse."

"It's what?" Kevin said, taking his eyes off the wolf and looking at Jade.

"You know," Tim said, lifting his shoulders to his ears. "Abstruse."

"Who are you kidding? You've got no idea what that means."

"Guys, are you in a relationship or what? It means puzzling, heavy, incomprehensible. Capeesh? Now let me think." She held up her finger to hush them. "We have completed a quantum jump into a parallel world. This is colossal." Jade spun around looking back at the wolf. "It can't touch us, it can't see us, and it looks like it can't hear or smell us any more. How long have you guys been able to do this? Is this some sort of experiment?" Jade was full of excitement and wonder at the expanding possibilities, her mind racing. Suddenly the joy in her face turned solemn. "Are we dead?"

"Why do you think you're dead?" Kevin asked.

"I thought we were dead too," Tim interjected.

"I saw Great Turtle — my great-grandmother was known as Great Turtle. She's dead. She is in the spirit world."

"We're not dead," Kevin said.

"Then we are in a *quantum* time and space, a parallel

universe, perhaps." Jade lit up like a Christmas tree. "I feel like the menorah on the eighth day of Hanukkah. This," she said, twirling around with her arms open, "my mother would have a field day with. Look at these plants. They appear to be soulful and alive." Gently, she brought her hand up under a soft leaf that was twice her hand size and touched it.

"That's one way to express it," Kevin said.

"How did you find this place?" she asked, letting the leaf down slowly. How did you open the passageway? I have so many questions."

"I think, first — first we should get home." Nervous, Kevin cleared his throat. "I think my mom might be able to help. She can come across as a real cranky person, but I feel we need her."

"Will she drive me home?" Jade asked.

"Sure," Kevin said.

"Okay, let's go see the dragon lady." Jade walked slowly, tilting her head back, gazing high up into the giant trees. "This is marvelous, absolutely marvelous," she said. "How many places have you been to?"

"Wait till you see the crystal cave."

"I'm lost as it is," Kevin said. "But to answer your question, this is the second time. Well, third, including now."

Kevin dropped behind and listened to Tim and Jade talking. She seemed intrigued and confused all at once by what they were saying.

Kevin allowed his thoughts to drift back to the day the boy drowned, wondering if he had opened a doorway then, and hadn't realized it. He remembered the details clearly:

riding his bike around the block testing the brakes, he had gone off-road down the track to the river. *I stopped to adjust the front end by placing the wheel between my legs and aligning the handlebars. When I found a cherry protein bar in my pocket, I ate it. What next, what next? I leant my bike on a tree near the river and took a leak.* He had looked into the river and watched the ripples on the surface floating in to the shore. Hypnotized by the rhythm he had taken off his shirt, and shallow-dived into the tiny waves, swimming underwater and holding his breath as long as he possibly could. He had surfaced and that's when he saw the boy upstream on a wooden bridge as it collapsed. Kevin had seen the boy clawing at the wood as it plummeted into the raging water. He could see the torrents as if they had been rushing his way but they never arrived. He had dived under, searching for the boy, thinking, *Nothing makes sense; there was no bridge.*

Breathless, he had surfaced into calm waters and the small sandy inlet before him. His bike had been leaning against the tree were he had left it. Quickly picking up his things, he had expected the water to still rise up behind him and over the sand and flood way beyond the trees. He had taken off on his bike, and waited. Nothing had happened, he had waited a little longer, but still nothing had happened. Balancing the bike between his legs, he had put his shirt on, then ridden off back to the river. Standing on the pedals he had craned his neck trying to see as much as possible before he actually got there.

Nothing … the river had been sleepy, gently lapping against the sandy shore.

He had listened for the roar of the torrents of water,

but there was no sound, except for some cicadas chirruping. He had propped his bike against the same tree and walked to the water's edge; nothing. He had jumped back onto his bike and coasted up along the river to where he thought he had seen the boy. There had been no bridge, no raging rapids, and no boy. He wasn't sure what he had actually seen, but the boy was real and his fear was real. Kevin had felt him gasping for air, his lungs being crushed.

What the hell! Kevin had thought, speeding home. His parents had called the police and they had found nothing and said he was crying wolf. *Maybe when I dove under the water, I arrived in a different time and place.* Abruptly, Kevin remembered there was someone else watching the boy drown, a pale girl with blonde hair watching from the other side.

Kevin didn't realize Tim and Jade had stopped walking. He would like to experiment with opening and closing the doorway like Jade has suggested. But how to start?

"He does this often. Earth to Kevin, Earth to Kevin." Tim stopped in front of Kevin, so that his friend crashed right into him.

"Sorry, man, you said something?"

"No, but I think you did, K," Tim said tapping the side of his head.

Kevin's face went red; he let his hair flop over his left eye. "Oh, shit, how embarrassing."

"We can still hear you," Jade said. "This is —" Quickly she tried to think of a word to dumb it down for them. It was hard to think of something simple.

"No way! You didn't just say 'dumb it down'?" Kevin looked askance.

"You can hear me?" Jade was shocked and even more excited than before. "This is phenomenal!"

Eyebrows raised, together the boys said, "Yep."

"This just keeps getting better and better." She reached behind and pulled her shorts out of her butt. "Give me a pair of cargoes any day," she said red-faced.

Kevin couldn't help watching as she tied her hair back, and wiped her face on her shirt. *She is simply beautiful.*

"Okay, stop there. We need some protocol here, guys. Like mind your thoughts."

Jade wasn't sure about these two, but they seemed harmless enough. Tim's sort of funny. Kevin has a crop of hair he's forever pushing out of his eyes or flipping to the side. If it bothers him that much, why doesn't he get a haircut? He's mysteriously amazing. Not too talkative, but he thinks a lot. He looks down at the ground most of the time as if lost in his own emotions. But he looks strong, muscular, athletic, and has a warm smile. "You know who you look like?" she said to Kevin. "River Phoenix."

"Seriously, who's checking out whom now?" Kevin said. "We heard all your thoughts just then."

"Who's he?" Tim asked.

"An actor from long ago who allegedly died of a drug overdose."

"Great! So Kevin looks like an actor who is on drugs."

"No, that's not what I meant. My mom and I watched a movie he was in, and she said he was a promising actor, very handsome in a rugged way. She had a crush on him when she was young."

"Nice save — I think," Tim said.

"When you said my name back there," she said to Kevin, "you said it as if you knew me."

"I had a vision of a deer and heard your name."

"A vision of a deer, and you heard my name. You're messing with me, right? This isn't real. I'm dreaming, aren't I? Great Turtle would have loved you. You had a vision." Jade laughed merrily.

"It's true. The deer led us to you," Kevin said.

"What happened to the boy who drowned? Did they ever find him?"

"No, and I don't want to talk about it."

"Then you'd better not think about it," she said.

The trio reached the cave and walked through it. Jade was entranced by the flickering crystals embedded in the walls. "I would love to take some samples but it feels inappropriate, the whole place seems to be breathing."

Together they emerged from behind the waterfall. Jade was in love with everything she saw. "A pink waterfall." She put her hand out and chuckled before putting her lips to the tiny pool in her palm. It tasted so sweet and clean, she just didn't know how to describe it. The water glided down the back of her throat and into the pit of her empty stomach; it felt like there were microscopic love butterflies gently calming and caressing her internals. "I feel so relaxed," she said. "This is so wonderful. It looks like a colorful painting done with cream, icing sugar, coconut and jelly. I just want to eat it all."

Tim turned to look back at her. "First, you want to

take samples, and then you think it's like a painting, and now you want to eat everything."

"Come on, we have to move," Kevin said, "time is ticking on. We need to find where we started from. It can't be far now."

"Hello!" Tim said. "There's the wall and our bikes." He pointed into the distance. The trees and leaves parted, creating a path for them. "Why couldn't you have created that an hour ago?"

"Stop saying that. I didn't create anything."

Wow, I don't want to leave. I want to stay, Jade thought.

"That's how I feel, too," Kevin said.

Enjoy this book? You can make a big difference

Reviews are the most powerful tools in my arsenal when it comes getting attention for my books. Much as I'd like to, I don't have the financial muscle of a New York publisher. I can't take out full page ads in the newspaper or put posters on the subway.

(Not yet, anyway).

But I do have something much more powerful and effective. A committed and loyal bunch of readers.

Honest reviews of my books help bring them to the attention of other readers.

If you've enjoyed this Part one of The Emerald Tablet: Book one in the Chronicles of the Supernatural, I would be very grateful if you could spend a few minutes leaving a review on your favorite online bookstore. And If you've enjoyed this Part one of The Emerald Tablet: Book one in the Chronicles of the Supernatural you can access The complete book THE EMERALD TABLET AND BOOK TWO REALM OF LOST SOULS AT https:// jmhartwriter.com/buy-now/

Thank you very much.

GLOSSARY

Al-mawet – Mawet means death, al-mawet is no death. The spelling varies within different religious text, but they all have the same meaning.

Arrow of time – the direction of events; movement in time is generally forward.

Athanasia – means timelessness, everlasting life. Athanasia is referred to as the parallel world/dimension.

Dark matter – a negative energy force. In this story the dark matter also contains micro shapeshifting demons.

Dovesti zhenshchinu – pronunciation for Russian довести женщину. English translation: bring the woman.

Dunny – toilet.

Fair dinkum – an expression in Australian slang proclaiming a truth about a statement.

Intel – slang for intelligent person. As in geek. (Created by the author)

Merkaba – two tetrahedrons combined. Mystically it

is a channel for the descending energy of the universe and the ascending energy of Earth. Spiritual tool of transformation.

Metatron's Cube – a geometric shape/solid. It has thirteen equal circles. Lines from the center of each circle extend out to the centers of the other 12 circles.

Outback – A remote area of the country.

Platonic Solids – shapes with equal sides. The five platonic solids are; tetrahedron hexahedron, octahedron, dodecahedron and icosahedron.

S=k log W – the second law of thermodynamics. Entropy – a mathematical formula that represents the lack of order or predictability. A slow decline into disorder or randomness. (Our characters want to reverse this state of being or create a new one from the disorder the negative thoughts of man and the micro beasts have created.)

Sphere – a round solid with equal distance from its center.

Stickybeak – an overly inquisitive person.

Talking stick – a ceremonial stick that is passed around a group of people giving the holder the right to speak.

The devil's puppets – the people controlled by the micro demons. Those infected by the virus which is the dark matter.

The Tree of Life – a spiritual concept that has been used and referred to throughout the centuries in mythology, religion and philosophy to name but a few. It refers to the interconnection of life and its evolution.

Vremaya dlya distsipliny – Russian pronunciation for Время для дисциплины. English translation: time for discipline (a good whipping in this story).

If you enjoyed the first book in the Emerald Tablet Series, please go to www.jmhartwriter.com for the next book.

ACKNOWLEDGMENT

I would like to thank my high school English teacher and my supportive family and friends for their encouragements. Thank you, to the invaluable editors, Linda Funnell and Stephanie Smith who have been a tremendous support. No book is complete without the vital service of editors, proofreaders and great book cover designers. Finally, I would like to acknowledge the professional project management services of Joel Naoum from Critical Mass, who made it possible to share my story with you.

ABOUT JM HART

Semi-retired, JM moved to a peaceful county town south
of Sydney, to focus on her grandchildren and writing.
JM Hart is the author of The Emerald Tablet Series, and
The Chronicles of the Supernatural. She makes her
online home at http://jmhartwriter.com
Pinterest
Facebook, Instagram and twitter, see links below.
And you should send her an email at
author@jmhartwriter.com if the mood strikes you.

BOOK THREE THE LEVIATHAN is due to be released
in JUNE 2020 AND BOOK FOUR coming out
NOVEMBER 2020 please visit website for more details.

facebook.com/JM-Hart-Writer-208264706568204
twitter.com/JMHartWriter
instagram.com/jmhartwriter
pinterest.com/jmhartwriter

First published by JMH World Publishing in 2018
This edition published in 2018 by JMH World Publishing
Copyright © JM Hart 2018
jmhartwriter.com

The Emerald Tablet SERIAL: Shadows of Doubt PART ONE
EPUB: 9781925786163
ISBN: 9780648558026
Cover design by Juan Padron

www.ingramcontent.com/pod-product-compliance
Lightning Source LLC
Chambersburg PA
CBHW030637110726
47901CB00002B/478

* 9 7 8 0 6 4 8 5 5 8 0 2 6 *